YEARLING BOOKS

P9-AQB-500

Since 1966, Yearling has been the

leading name in classic and award-winning

literature for young readers.

With a wide variety of titles,

Yearling paperbacks entertain, inspire,

and encourage a love of reading.

OTHER YEARLING BOOKS YOU WILL ENJOY

ME, MOP, AND THE MOONDANCE KID
Walter Dean Myers

THE WAR WITH GRANDPA, *Robert Kimmel Smith*

THE SLAVE DANCER, *Paula Fox*

JACKSON JONES AND MISSION GREENTOP
Mary Quattlebaum

JACKSON JONES AND THE PUDDLE OF THORNS
Mary Quattlebaum

OUT OF PATIENCE, *Brian Meehl*

LIZZIE BRIGHT AND THE BUCKMINSTER BOY
Gary D. Schmidt

walter dean myers

Darnell Rock Reporting

A YEARLING BOOK

Published by Yearling, an imprint of Random House Children's Books
a division of Random House, Inc., New York

Copyright © 1994 by Walter Dean Myers

Visit us on the Web! www.randomhouse.com/kids

Educators and librarians, for a variety of teaching tools, visit us at
www.randomhouse.com/teachers

Library of Congress Cataloging-in-Publication Data is available on request.

ISBN: 978-0-440-41157-4

Reprinted by arrangement with Delacorte Press

Printed in the United States of America

March 1996

35 34 33 32 31 30 29 28 27

To the Corner Crew
Charles Culler Middle School
in Lincoln, Nebraska

ONE

"Yo! You're changing the channels so fast I can't see what's on!" Thirteen-year-old Darnell Rock was lying on the sofa, looking over his twin sister's shoulder.

"Yo yourself!" said Tamika. She kept the remote control just out of her brother's reach as she raced through the channels. "If you want to see what's on, you got to look faster."

"How can you look faster?"

"I don't know, but it's not my problem," Tamika said. "And didn't Mama tell you to clean the living room?"

"It's already clean," Darnell said. From where he lay on the couch, he straightened out the magazines in the rack and turned the carved mahogany elephant that sat in the middle of the coffee table so that it faced the television.

"I know you didn't dust." Tamika had sparkling white teeth and a wide smile that brightened her whole face. Her dark eyes twinkled. She knew that Darnell had not even thought about dusting.

"You got it made with putting the garbage out," Darnell said.

"That's life, baby." Tamika laughed. It was her job to separate the family's garbage, to drop the regular garbage down the garbage chute in the hallway of their apartment building, and to put out the recyclables in the hallway on Mondays and Wednesdays.

Darnell looked a lot like his sister, except that he was just a little lighter in complexion. He was the same coffee-brown tone as his mother, while Tamika was dark, like their father. Another difference was that Tamika had the fastest smile in the entire city of Oakdale. If she wasn't really mad or feeling terrible, she would find something to smile about. Darnell, on the other hand, didn't smile unless something was really funny or at least made him feel good.

"I bet you were adopted," Darnell said. "I can't figure you to be anybody's natural sister."

"Oh, shut up, Darnell."

"That's why our names are so different. If we were really twins they would have named us something like Darnell and Donna, or Darnell and Darnellette."

"In the first place, I never heard of anybody named Darnellette," Tamika said. "And you heard Mommy say a hundred times that she didn't want to hook us up with those stupid twin names."

"I still think they either adopted you or won you in one of those games where you break a balloon and get a prize."

Tamika pointed the remote at her brother and clicked the channel changer.

"What's all this noise going on in here?" Sidney

Rock came into the living room, pushed Darnell's legs off the couch, and sat down heavily. He ran his fingers along the side of his head through what was left of his hair and tried to push it toward the bald spot on top of his head.

"Your youngest child has got a problem because I won't let him hold the remote control," Tamika said. She was always reminding Darnell that he had been born six minutes after her.

"I'll settle it," Mr. Rock said. "Give me the changer."

"You're as bad as she is," Darnell said. "You keep switching channels, too."

"Watch your mouth, boy." Mr. Rock eased off his shoes and put his feet up on the coffee table.

"You work hard today, Daddy?" Tamika asked.

"Always working hard," Mr. Rock said. "Why don't you either put the news on or give me the remote."

Tamika flipped the remote to her father. He caught it in midair with one hand. "How was school?" he said to no one in particular as he started clicking the remote.

"Okay except for the mass murders and the kangaroo in the lunchroom," Tamika said.

"That's good," Mr. Rock said.

"Yo, Daddy, she's messing with you again," Darnell said. "You didn't hear what she said."

Mr. Rock looked at Tamika and asked her when she was going to grow up. "You're almost—"

"Fourteen," Tamika added. "In February."

"Yeah," Mr. Rock said as he changed channels. "You got to be acting more mature."

"She's always messing with somebody," Darnell said. "This guy got arrested in the supermarket today and she had to mess with him."

"What was he arrested for?"

"He was trying to shoplift a potato," Darnell said. "They had him in handcuffs and Tamika went up to the guy and asked him if he was going to jail."

"A potato?" Sidney Rock put the television on mute.

"Yeah, he was one of those homeless guys that hang out on McGinley Square," Darnell said.

"He shouldn't have been shoplifting," Tamika said. "I'm glad they caught him. Then he had the nerve to get nasty, too."

"What did he say?" Mr. Rock asked.

"Said we were rich kids who forgot what it was like being colored," Tamika said. "I told him at least we didn't steal potatoes."

"You shouldn't have been talking to him at all," Mr. Rock said. "He could have been dangerous."

Darnell thought of the man. He had two jackets under the dark overcoat he wore. Standing in front of the cat food display, his hands cuffed behind his back, he had looked more uncomfortable than dangerous. He had kept looking up at the ceiling, and his mouth opened and closed as if he were just ready to say something, but nothing had come out until Tamika had spoken to him.

"How long do you think he'll stay in jail?" Darnell asked.

"Probably just overnight," his father said, still looking at the television screen. "They don't have room in the jails for people stealing potatoes. He might have got caught on purpose to have someplace to stay. People do things like that."

It was Darnell's mother who had decided to have leftovers on Mondays. It was a way not to waste food, she said. When she called them to the table it was full of small dishes, including fried chicken and collard greens from Sunday dinner, tuna salad from Saturday lunch, meatballs, and an assortment of vegetables.

"Eat what you want, but make sure you eat something green." Linda Rock walked for an hour at the mall three days a week and was in great shape. Her face was round, with large eyes that were spaced wide apart, and full lips that she touched lightly with lip gloss.

"I can see this little traffic cop in your stomach telling the food where to go," Tamika said. "Green to the left, orange to the right. What other color is food?"

"How much is a potato, anyway?" Darnell asked.

"How many calories?" his mother asked.

"No. How much money?"

"One medium potato should weigh about a third of a pound," his mother said. "So if a pound of potatoes costs sixty cents, then one potato would cost about twenty cents."

"Then we saw somebody going to jail over less than a quarter," Darnell said.

"You saw somebody going to jail over stealing

something from the supermarket," Mr. Rock said. "The cost doesn't mean anything."

It was Tamika who jumped in with the entire story, including the part about the man saying that they were rich kids who had forgotten how to be colored.

Darnell didn't think that the man really thought that he and Tamika were rich. He was embarrassed, that was all. He had an old-looking face, but Darnell had the impression that the man wasn't that old, not really.

"Compared to some people," his mother was saying, "we are rich. Your father has a good job at the post office and I do all right at the department store."

"Two people willing to work," his father said. "You want that meatball?"

His father was pointing at the last meatball with his pointer finger, which was short and stumpy.

"No, I don't want it," Darnell said.

"He thinks if he eats too many meatballs he's going to get fat," Tamika said. "Then Paula Snow won't like him."

"What do I care if she likes me?" Darnell said. "I don't like her!"

"The only reason you joined the school newspaper is so you could be next to her and her greasy sandwiches," Tamika went on. "She brings these greasy sandwiches in an old paper bag every day, but Darnell is in love with her so he don't mind."

"You need to be punched right in your nose," Darnell said.

"You're going to be on the newspaper?" Mrs. Rock asked, surprised. "That's very nice, Darnell."

"Maybe," Darnell said. "I'll check it out."

"And check out Paula Snow," Tamika said.

"Yo, Tamika, why don't you do something creative, you know, like shutting up?"

"That's enough fighting at the dinner table," Mrs. Rock said, wiping her hands with a paper towel. "Now, Tamika, apologize to your brother."

"Oh, Darnell, I'm sooo sorry," Tamika said in a way that nobody in the whole world would believe that she was sorry.

"And Darnell"—Mrs. Rock put her elbows on the table, leaned forward, and placed her chin on her fists—"tell me about this new girlfriend."

"Mom!"

Darnell was glad that his mother was kidding him about Paula Snow. It was better than having her asking him about the newspaper. He hadn't done his homework last week and was sitting in the principal's office when Mr. Baker had said he was disgusted with him.

"Can't you spend one day without getting into trouble?" the principal asked him.

Darnell had put his head down and shrugged, hoping that Mr. Baker wouldn't tell him to bring his parents in again.

"If you can't do anything positive, why are you coming to school?"

"To learn," Darnell had answered.

"To learn? To learn *what*? Your grades are terrible,

your behavior is terrible, and you don't do one thing for this school!''

"I was thinking of joining the school newspaper," he had said, remembering the announcement they had made over the loudspeaker that morning.

"You?" Mr. Baker looked at him with his head to one side. "Am I hearing right?"

"Yes, sir." Darnell tried to remember the whole announcement, but couldn't think of anything more than that it was being run by Mr. Derby.

"Okay, Darnell," Mr. Baker said. "I'm going to see if you do anything on the school paper. But if you don't get yourself straight soon, I'm going to have to speak to your parents and maybe even suggest they try another school for you."

He hadn't told anybody what Mr. Baker had said, not even Tamika, and surely not his parents.

Before it became a middle school, South Oakdale was the town's oldest high school. Larry Keyes, Darnell's best friend, said that the red brick building was so old that George Washington once dropped by and borrowed an ax from the shop class to cut down a cherry tree.

"They made it a prison for a little while," Larry said. "That's why the windows are so small, so the prisoners can't get out. Then once they were sure that the building wasn't fit for kids, they made it into a middle school."

It was September, and there were a lot of new kids at South Oakdale, so there was a lot to look at as Larry and Darnell headed toward the corner near the gym. Larry was exactly the same height as Darnell but looked a lot bigger because he was heavy and had shoulders that were straight and wide. He looked like a tough kid, but he had a little high voice that reminded everybody of the Chipmunks. He was funny, too. At least he was funny most of the time. His parents were divorced, and when he thought about that he wasn't funny at all.

"I heard that if you go down in the basement," Larry went on, bobbing his head as he walked, "you can still find the bodies of some high school kids who were on detention."

"What gets me about detention," Darnell said, "is that you can't do anything when you get it. You just have to sit there."

"I don't like it at all," Larry said. They were approaching the school from the rear. There was a basketball game going on, and they changed their direction to get a better look.

"Did I say I liked it?" Darnell asked. "Did I say I liked it? All I said was that it is even worse because you can't do anything except sit there and be stupid."

"If they had you doing something it would probably be something like breaking up rocks or something like you were on a chain gang," Larry said.

"Here comes Freddy," Darnell said. "I didn't think he was going to South Oakdale."

"They letting anybody in now," Larry said.

They watched as Freddy Haskell cut across the lawn toward them. The collar of the white shirt he wore was crumpled, the way his collars always were, and the tie was off to one side.

"Hi, Larry. Hi, Darnell," Freddy said with a wave of his hand. He stopped a few feet in front of Larry and Darnell.

"You talking to seventh-graders, man," Larry said. "When a sixth-grader speaks to a seventh-grader he's supposed to say Mister. You can call us Mister Larry and Mister Darnell."

"Aw, man . . ." Freddy smiled.

"What you mean, 'Aw, man'!" Darnell tried to lower his voice but it just sounded a little hoarse. "He said you got to call us Mister. He didn't say anything about no 'Aw, man.' "

Freddy waved his hand and started away.

"Next time you see us you better call us Mister," Larry yelled at him.

"He's so neat I bet his mama irons his underwear," Darnell said.

"He's okay, though," Larry said. "Just too neat."

"That's catchy, too," Darnell said. "You hang around him for a few hours and you find yourself wanting to get neat. One day he walked me all the way down to Terry Street and I got this urge to go in and put on a tie."

"I got to stay away from him, then," Larry said. "Hey, you want to play basketball after school?"

"Can't," Darnell said. "Got a meeting of the newspaper people."

"You like that newspaper stuff?" Larry asked.

"How do I know?" Darnell asked. "They're just having their first meeting today. I'll tell you one thing, though. If it's like homework, or something like that, I'm quitting."

"If it was me," Larry said, rubbing the end of his nose with his palm, "I'd quit right away."

TWO

★ "South Oakdale has had a newspaper just about every other year," Mr. Derby said. "It all depends on how many kids are really interested in the paper at the beginning of the school year and how many stay with it. We really need at least eight people to put out a decent paper."

"We got ten!" said Tony O'Casio. He had dark eyes and heavy eyebrows that moved up and down as he spoke. Everything in the school seemed to excite him.

Darnell looked around as Mr. Derby counted the kids. There were ten, as Tony had said. There were two kids Darnell had never seen before, and he figured them to be sixth-graders.

"Okay, we're going to meet two days a week, Wednesdays and Fridays," Mr. Derby went on. The history teacher was tall, with almost white hair even though he was one of the younger teachers. "If you can't make a meeting, please call someone and find out what happened. What I want you to do is to think of the *Gazette* staff as a team. Every time we put out a good newspaper, we win."

"We're going to use the computer?" one of the kids Darnell didn't know asked.

"Yes, but first I want everyone to introduce themselves," Mr. Derby said. "And if you think you know what you would like to do on the paper, now would be a good time to bring it up. We'll start with Tony."

"Okay." Tony's fingers were drumming nervously on the desk as he spoke. "My name is Tony O'Casio, but everyone calls me Tony 'O,' and that's the name I'm going to have on my column. Mostly I'm interested in sports."

"I never heard anyone call you Tony 'O,' " Paula said.

"Who asked you?" Tony asked.

"Go on, Paula."

"My name is Paula Snow, I'm in the seventh grade, and I'm interested in being a reporter," Paula said. Paula was dark and pretty and got the best grades in the school.

Kitty Gates was next. She was the second-tallest girl in the school, and some of the guys used to call her Skinny Minny because she was so thin. You could always tell how she felt because when she was happy she had a very wide smile and when she was sad she looked as if she was just about ready to cry.

"My name is Eddie Latimer, I'm in the seventh grade, and I want to take pictures."

"You have a camera, don't you, Eddie?" Mr. Derby asked.

"He's got three cameras," Mark volunteered.

"Yo, man, I don't need you to answer my questions," Eddie said. Eddie was shorter than most of the guys in the school, but he had enormous eyes and he could draw as well as take pictures. "I have four cameras," he said. "But one of them is broken. I got sand in it."

Mark Robbins was an eighth-grader with a round face that some girls thought was handsome. He was smart, but he talked so fast that sometimes it was hard to understand him. He said that he could do anything on a newspaper. "I can lay the paper out, or I can do reporting . . . anything," he said.

Darnell was next, and he tried to think of what he was going to say. Mr. Derby looked at him as Mark was finishing. Darnell knew that the principal, Mr. Baker, had asked Mr. Derby to take him on the *Gazette* staff.

"I understand you're interested in sports, too," Mr. Derby said.

"Yeah," Darnell said.

"What's your name?" Angie Cruz asked.

"You know my . . . my name is Darnell Rock, and I'm interested in just being on the paper," Darnell said. "What's your name?"

"My name is Angelica Cruz." The pretty Puerto Rican girl took off her glasses. She was cream-colored with soft brown eyes and hair that she wore combed out and down her back. "And I would like to write either an advice column or news."

Everyone in the school knew Linda Gold. If there was ever a list with kids who had done something or won something, you could always find Linda's name near the top of it. She was blond with gray-green eyes and a sprinkling of freckles around her nose. She also had a running battle with Miss Green, who accused her of violating the school rules by using lipstick.

Donald Williams and Jessica Lee turned out to be the two sixth-graders who had volunteered to work on the *Gazette* staff. Donald said he was eleven, but he looked as if he were ten, especially when he took off his glasses. He said his father worked in computers and he knew a lot about them.

Dark-haired Jessica Lee spoke with a slight accent. She said that she could draw.

"Are you Chinese or something?" Tony asked.

"I'm glad that you're curious about the people around you," Mr. Derby said. "But as a reporter you have to know how to ask questions, and when to ask them. You have to be careful not to offend people with the way you ask questions."

"Okay," Tony said. "My folks are from the Dominican Republic. Where are your folks from?"

"Taiwan," Jessica said.

"Fine, that was good," Mr. Derby said. "I'm glad to see that most of you have specific interests, but we're going to find that we have to do a lot of different jobs to get a newspaper out each month. What we're going to do today is to choose some assignments and maybe talk about what we want in the first issue."

"I'll be the sports guy," Tony said. "Tony O! on sports. That's an 'O' with an exclamation point."

"We'll start with editor," Mr. Derby said, ignoring

Tony. "The editor in chief more or less runs the paper, and makes assignments. Now, is there anybody here who wants to be editor in chief?"

Darnell watched as seven hands went into the air. He had thought about being the person who wrote about sports, but Tony had spoken up first.

"I always get good marks in English," Linda Gold said.

"So do I." Mark Robbins always looked as if he had a smile on his face, even when he wasn't smiling. "Are we going to go by marks?"

"I think we should go by who wants to be the editor," Eddie Latimer said. "And since just about everybody wants to be the editor, let's have a vote and get on with it."

"Is that what you call great English?" Linda asked.

"Voting's a good idea," Mr. Derby said. He passed out three-by-five cards. "Put down your choice of editor, and we'll count them. But remember, we're voting for the person who's probably going to get stuck doing more work than anyone else."

He wrote down the names of the seven candidates on the board, and everyone voted by writing a name on the card and turning it in to Mr. Derby.

Mr. Derby read off the votes as he added them up. "Jennifer, one. Linda, one. Linda, two. Mark, one. Donald, one. Kitty, one. Kitty, two. Kitty, three. Angie, one. Kitty, four. Looks like Kitty will be our new editor."

"Way to go, Kitty!" Angie Cruz was the only one who looked happy with the outcome of the voting.

Kitty Gates was nice but very quiet. Darnell had

been to her birthday party two years ago, mostly because his mother had made him go.

"Okay, how about making me the official photographer?" Eddie said.

"Is that okay?" Kitty asked Mr. Derby.

"Sure, if it's okay with you," Mr. Derby said.

"And Tony will be sports writer," Kitty said.

"Naturally," Tony said.

"I've got an idea for a column," Angie Cruz spoke up. "I could do something on what people are talking about around the school."

"Fine," Kitty said.

"Suppose nobody's talking about anything?" Mark said.

"Then I'll do something and write about that," Angie said.

Then Mr. Derby wanted to know what the first lead story was going to be. Everybody looked at Kitty and she didn't look particularly bright.

"What do you think?" she asked, looking around at everybody. "Do you know any news?"

"A dog got into the library last week," Donald said.

"That's not important enough for our first issue," Kitty said.

"Hey, it's news," Mark said. "We're supposed to print anything that's news."

"No, we're not," Kitty said, looking over toward Mr. Derby. "We're supposed to figure out what kind of newspaper we're going to be."

"How about a paper," Eddie Latimer said, "that prints stories about dogs that come to school?"

"How about world peace?" Kitty said.

"Give me a break!" Linda was still mad about not being editor, and she showed it. "What are we going to do about world peace?"

"Write about it!" Donald said.

"So world peace will be the focus of our first issue," Mr. Derby said. He stood up and they knew the meeting was over. "I want everybody to pick up copies of the old school newspapers from my office sometime this week. And I want everybody to make sure they read at least one regular newspaper each day."

Kitty told the staff to go around and interview students and teachers about world peace. Darnell felt good about being on the staff, but he didn't want to go around talking to students because he didn't want anybody getting on his case about being on the paper, especially Chris McKoy. Chris, besides being the toughest boy in the school, was the unofficial head of the Corner Crew.

The Corner Crew had been started the year before when Mr. Thrush, the gym teacher, had caught some kids, including Darnell, hanging out on the corner after the late bell had rung. They were all put on detention, but the next week, when the same kids were on the same corner, they were sent to Mr. Baker's office. Mr. Baker really got on their case.

"You young people have to learn to participate in school activities," he had said. "You won't get anywhere in life hanging out on the corner."

But it was Miss Seldes, the school librarian, who had first called them Oakdale's official Corner Crew.

When she found out that the kids were friends, she had asked Mr. Baker for permission to have them meet in the library.

For Darnell, the idea of an official Corner Crew and having meetings was strange. They weren't having meetings on the corner, they just happened to hang out there sometimes. They tried to explain that to Miss Seldes, but she didn't seem to catch on. Or maybe she did. She arranged with Mr. Baker that they would be allowed to meet in the library anytime after school and told them they could do anything they wanted as long as they didn't hurt school property. She had even had T-shirts made up for them that read "SOCC," for South Oakdale Corner Crew.

The thing about the Corner Crew was that mostly they weren't into anything special. Darnell thought they were just ordinary, but Mr. Baker said that they were the kind of kids who fell through cracks. Darnell hadn't liked the remark, but Mr. Baker didn't seem to notice. It wasn't that he was trying not to participate in anything, he thought; it just turned out that way. Chris McKoy, on the other hand, just didn't like anything; that was the way he was. Darnell didn't even think he liked himself. The other members of the Corner Crew were Tamika; Sonia Burrows, who was cool but stayed out of school a lot; Darnell's best friend, Larry; and Benny Quiros. Benny was dark Spanish and had shaved his head on one side. He wore an earring for a while, but then Mr. Baker made a rule against it.

Another thing about the Cornor Crew was that

most of them, including Darnell, weren't doing that well in school. Miss Seldes said the fact that they didn't participate in much around the school was one of the reasons they didn't get good grades. Miss Seldes wore small granny glasses, long skirts, and an array of ribbons in her dark hair that changed the way she looked, depending on what ribbons she had found that morning. She seemed always to have something on her mind that she couldn't put aside. She asked Darnell to stay with the Corner Crew for a while.

"I don't want to join nothing stupid!" Tamika had said on the way home.

"You could get some better marks," Darnell answered.

"A Corner Crew sounds like you're supposed to be picking up garbage or something," Tamika had said. "Why do you want to be on it?"

"She said she can get us out of detention," Darnell said. "That's something."

"I'd stay in it permanently," Tamika had answered, "if she got me a lavender blouse."

"That is so stupid," Darnell said.

"Ain't it?"

THREE

"So why do I have to do it?" Darnell asked, looking at Kitty. It was the day after the first meeting of the *Gazette* staff, and Darnell had met some of the other staff members in the hallway.

"Because I assigned you to do it," Kitty said. "If the editor in chief assigns you to a story, you have to do it."

"Hey, as much time as you spend in the principal's office it should be easy for you to interview Mr. Baker," Mark said.

"Yo, Mark, shut up!" Darnell gave Mark a look that let him know he meant business.

"And you're not doing it alone," Linda said. "You and I are going to interview him."

"Yeah, well, you better ask all the questions," Darnell said.

Interviewing Mr. Baker was not what Darnell thought being on the newspaper was going to be about. And having to do the interview with Linda Gold was no big deal. Linda was the kind of girl who seemed to do everything right. Darnell could easily imagine her getting out of bed early in the morning and answering math questions as she brushed her teeth.

His next class was English, and he had to listen to Mrs. Finley talk about a story about an old man who went fishing. Chris McKoy was in the class, being stupid as usual.

"So how come"—Chris was looking around the class to see who was looking at him—"he wrote a story about this guy when he didn't do anything?"

"He caught the fish," Lee Chiang said from the back of the class, "but then the other fish got it."

"So he should have written about the other fish," Chris said.

"It's his story," Lee said. "He can write about what he wants to."

"But Chris wants to know why he chose to write about the old man losing the fish," Mrs. Finley said. "Why do you think the author wrote this story?"

Mrs. Finley's question sounded like something she would have on a test, and Darnell thought about writing it down.

"Maybe the old man was a chump," Chris said. "And he wanted to show up a chump."

"Do you really believe that, Chris?" Mrs. Finley asked.

"Yeah," Chris answered as the bell rang.

Mrs. Finley told the class to read the next fifteen pages in the book. Darnell noticed that Chris was the first one out the door.

There were two kinds of classes at Oakdale: Plateau and Ladder. The Plateau classes were for kids who were on the right reading level. The Ladder classes were for kids reaching toward their reading level. Darnell was in a Ladder class, but he was pretty sure that he was going to be in a Plateau class the next year. Mrs. Finley had told him that he was already close.

There were two lunch periods, and usually Darnell ate in the first one, but Mr. Derby had arranged for the interview with Mr. Baker now. He went to the principal's office and stood outside.

Tamika was going by and stopped. "What did you do?" she asked.

"Nothing," Darnell said.

"Again?" Tamika shook her head and started down the hall.

A moment later Linda Gold showed up with a notebook and a pencil in her hand. Darnell wished he had thought to bring along a notebook.

"I'll introduce us," Linda said, "then you ask him how long he's been principal, and I'll ask him the rest of the questions. Okay?"

"Yeah, okay." Darnell felt unsure of himself as they walked into the outer office.

There was a long counter just inside the office. Behind the counter there were two desks. Miss Green sat behind one of them, and Mr. Thrush used the other one when he wasn't doing his gym stuff.

"Hello, Linda." Miss Green smiled at Linda. "Sit on the bench, Darnell—and keep quiet."

"Hey, I'm not on suspension," Darnell said with a scowl.

"We're here from the school newspaper to interview Mr. Baker," Linda said.

"Oh." Miss Green looked at Darnell and shrugged. She dialed Mr. Baker and then told Linda and Darnell to go into his office.

Mr. Baker's office was large. His desk was big enough, but he also had a couch on one side with a small table in front of it. When parents came in he sat on the couch with them.

"We're from the *Gazette* staff," Linda started. "I'm Linda Gold, and I guess you know Darnell Rock."

"We've met," Mr. Baker said, leaning back in his chair.

Linda nudged Darnell with her foot.

"How long have you been a principal?" Darnell asked.

"This is my seventh year," Mr. Baker said.

Darnell watched as Linda wrote down Mr. Baker's answer.

"What do you like about being a principal?" Linda asked.

"Well, I like the opportunity to help young people achieve their educational goals," Mr. Baker said. "There's nothing better than the introduction of the young to the pleasures of education. And when I say 'pleasures' I mean exactly that. A Greek philosopher once said that education is the purpose of the wise man, not just its use. When I was a young man, not much older . . ."

Mr. Baker's voice droned on and on and Darnell saw Linda writing furiously. Now he was glad he had forgotten to bring a notebook.

There was a fly in the office, and Darnell tried to keep track of it without Mr. Baker or Linda knowing what he was doing. The fly buzzed along the top of the window and then went to the flag behind Mr. Baker's desk.

"What goals do you have for the school?" Linda asked.

"Basically, my goals are for the individual students," Mr. Baker said. "I want each child who goes to South Oakdale Middle School to be excited about learning. School should be something they see as a pleasure, and also as a challenge. . . ."

The fly was on the wall, then made a lazy circle around Linda's head and then landed on Mr. Baker's arm. Darnell covered his mouth to hide his smile, but Mr. Baker saw it and gave him a stern look.

"Is there anything that you would like to say to the student body in the *Gazette*?" Linda asked.

"Only this"—Mr. Baker had the palms of his hands together and was looking up toward the ceiling—"that we are going through a partnership, a process, a celebration of exploration . . ."

The answer seemed as long as the others, and Darnell looked for the fly. He saw it on the corner of the desk. The fly wasn't moving, and Darnell thought that maybe it had been bored to death.

"Well, thank you for the interview." Linda was standing, and Darnell jumped to his feet.

"I'm always pleased to participate," Mr. Baker said. "And I'm glad to see Darnell in my office for a reason other than his behavior."

Outside in the hall, Linda said she was going to write up the interview.

"You wrote the whole thing down?" he asked.

"Not every word," Linda said. "That's not what reporters do. You just write down the high points."

"Like when we said good-bye?"

"Darnell, grow up!" Linda sucked her teeth as she went out the door.

"Hey, he didn't say nothing you didn't know he was going to say," Darnell said.

"That's not the point," Linda said. "He said it to the staff of the *Gazette,* and that makes it official. Now I have to go write the story up."

Official or not, Darnell knew he didn't think much of the interview.

FOUR

Darnell followed Linda to the room the *Gazette* was using for its office. She plopped down in front of the computer and switched it on.

"What do you think I should use as a title?" she asked.

"How's about 'Boring, Boring, Boring'?" Darnell sat at the teacher's desk and opened the side drawer. He tucked one foot in the drawer and the other on top of the desk.

"I'm probably going to have to do this all alone, so you might as well leave." Linda began to type up the interview.

"You might be right," Darnell said. He got up and looked over Linda's shoulder as she wrote.

"Darnell, I don't need your pizza-and-root-beer breath on my neck," Linda complained.

The door of the classroom opened, and Mr. Derby came in. "How did the interview go?"

"Darnell thinks our interview with Mr. Baker was boring, but he didn't ask any good questions and he's certainly not helping now," Linda said.

"Darnell . . ." Mr. Derby looked at Darnell and then away. "Linda, do the best you can," he said.

"I'll have it finished by tomorrow morning," Linda answered.

When Mr. Derby left, Darnell sat back down at the desk. He watched as Linda typed, taking her eyes from the keyboard to the monitor. He had a familiar feeling, something he couldn't quite put his finger on, but it was there nevertheless. Maybe, he thought, the newspaper wasn't for him after all. It was easy for someone to say that he should participate in school activities, but it wasn't easy to do. He looked at the window. It had begun to rain lightly, and small droplets of water made barely visible streaks on the dusty windowpanes.

"Later!" Darnell swung his feet to the ground and headed for the door.

On the corner, Chris was standing with Sonia. Darnell saw that Sonia had her books.

"You going home early?" he asked as he got near them.

"She hasn't been to school yet," Chris said.

"My mother had to go to court this morning," Sonia said. "So I had to baby-sit my brother. What are you doing out here? I thought you had turned over a new leaf."

"Just needed some air, I guess," Darnell said. "How come you just didn't stay home today?"

"Because Mr. Baker said if my attendance record gets any worse I'm out of the school," Sonia answered. "But I really don't want to hear his mouth, so maybe I won't go in after all."

"I saw you and Linda going in and interviewing Mr. Baker," Chris said. "How did it go?"

"I didn't know what to ask him," Darnell said. "Linda asked a lot of stupid stuff."

"Like what?" Chris asked.

"Like how he liked being a principal," Darnell said. "I figured if he didn't like it he wouldn't be doing it."

"We got to get back into school before Mr. Thrush comes out," Chris said. "You coming, Sonia?"

"Yeah." Sonia nodded as she spoke.

They went around to the side of the building and in through the side door.

After school, Larry had to go pay his mother's insurance and asked Darnell to go with him to the insurance office.

"Where's it at?" Darnell asked.

"Over on River Street."

"River Street?" Darnell looked at Larry. "You got moncy for carfare?"

"Sure," Larry said. "We can get the bus over on Montgomery Street."

"You want to walk and get some pizza on the way over there?" Darnell asked.

"No, 'cause I don't want to take the insurance money into the pizza place." Larry took out his headphones and put them around his neck.

"What you got on?" Darnell asked. "I bet you got one of them dumb tapes on."

"I'm listening to the speeches of Malcolm X."

Darnell snatched the headphones from around

Larry's neck and listened. He looked up and saw Larry's stupid grin. "That ain't no Malcolm. That's that dumb music your aunt bought for you!"

"So, it was free!" Larry said, taking back the headphones. "And the best things in life are free."

"No, they're not," Darnell said. "You always say that, but I know it's not true."

"The air is free."

"Yeah, but so are measles," Darnell said.

"I don't even know how you get measles." It was warm, and Larry opened his jacket. "There goes that crazy dude."

Darnell saw the tall brown man standing in front of the La Famosa bodega. He was standing in front of the window, looking at the cans of vegetables and talking to himself.

"I'll tell you how you get measles," Darnell said. "If somebody's got measles and they sneeze on you or something like that, then you'll get them."

"Anybody sneeze on me I'll punch them out," Larry said.

"Yeah, but you can't punch out a measle," Darnell said. "But maybe you can keep them away with that okeydokey music you be listening to."

"Man, it's okay."

There were eighteen blocks from school to the insurance company. If they had walked down Jackson it would have been through blocks where mostly African Americans lived. The blocks they passed walking toward River Street had once been all Italian but now they were mostly Spanish, and the streets were lined with small shops with signs in the windows in both English and Spanish. There were vendors on the street as well, and the smell of grilled sausages and onions filled the air. Some little kids from St. Bridget's, in their blue and gray uniforms, crowded around the entrance to a five-and-ten-cent store.

The insurance office was across from a bank, and they watched as two guards carried bags of money from an armored car through the bank's revolving doors. One of the guards had his gun out.

They went into the office and went to the counter, where Larry gave the clerk the notice his mother had received and a money order.

A thin white woman came in and came to the counter. The clerk put Larry's notice and money order down and turned her attention to the white woman.

"Hey, Larry, how come that woman got waited on before you?" Darnell asked.

"Yeah, I was here first," Larry said.

The clerk ignored them. The thin woman looked at Larry and smiled nervously. Larry smiled back.

It took them another ten minutes before the clerk had taken the money order from Larry, entered it on her computer, stamped a receipt, and given it to him. Outside it looked as if it might rain again.

"You shouldn't have smiled at that woman," Darnell said. "When she smiled at you you should have given her a mean look."

"I can't give people mean looks," Larry said. "Once I practiced giving out mean looks, but it didn't work."

"You practiced?"

"Yeah, in the mirror."

"No lie?"

"No lie!"

"That's what that stupid music does for you," Darnell said. "Takes away all your meanness."

Friday afternoons at South Oakdale were either great or terrible, but mostly they were great. Everybody was ready to chill out over the weekend and anxious to get started. It was only terrible if you had makeup homework to get done or Friday afternoon detention. Darnell was out the front door when he saw Eddie Latimer, a camera around his neck, pointing back into the building.

"We have a staff meeting in two minutes!" he said.

Darnell had forgotten about the meeting, and started not to go. But there was Eddie Latimer holding the door for him and talking about how they had to hurry.

When they got to the *Gazette* office they saw that Kitty had put up a big sign that said "Please Put All Story Ideas on the Board." There was one story idea pinned up. It was about the new gym floor and was signed by Angie Cruz.

"What new gym floor?" Tony O! asked.

If anybody in the world knew everything, it was Angie Cruz. The girl was in everybody's business. She was the one who broke the news that the gym was getting a new floor.

"It's going to be a professional basketball floor,"

Angie was saying. "Everybody's going to use the girls' gym for two weeks while they put it down. It's already made up in sections. They just have to bring it here and lay it down."

"Who told you that?" Tony O! asked, mad because he didn't know about the new gym floor.

"I have sources," Angie said, closing her eyes the way she did when she was pleased with herself. "And they're going to put up new baskets, the kind with the glass backboards, too."

"Hey, they're nice!" Donald was leaning against the wall. He spun an imaginary ball around his midsection twice and then put up an imaginary layup. "It's about time they fixed up that raggedy gym," he said.

"I'm going to interview Mr. Thrush," Tony O! said. "Darnell, you want to go with me?"

"No, he don't like me," Darnell said.

"That's no big deal," Tony O! said. "He doesn't like anybody. Come on."

Darnell thought that if anybody knew about Mr. Thrush it would be Tony O! He decided to go with him to interview Mr. Thrush.

There had been a newspaper story about Merle Thrush, and someone had framed it and put it in the trophy case in the main hallway. It said that he had played football in high school and college and had wrestled on an international team. Now he coached most of the sports at South Oakdale and was in charge of detention. His office was on the third floor, down from the girls' gym, and they caught him just as he was going to leave.

"Mr. Thrush!" Tony O! stood a foot away from the door and shouted into the athletic office. "Can we interview you for the school newspaper about the new gym?"

Mr. Thrush was stuffing a newspaper into an old briefcase. He looked up at the clock, then sat down in the swivel chair and motioned them in. Tony O! went into the office, and Darnell followed him.

"How come we're getting a new gym?" Tony O! asked.

"It's not a new gym, just a new floor." Merle Thrush *looked* like a coach to Darnell. His neck was almost as wide as his face, and he had a chin that stuck out like it was mad at something. "We had the money for the new backboards for a while, but I wanted to wait until we got the new floor. If we get the backboards and the floor from the same company, they'll throw in a new scoreboard."

"Hey, that's going to be on the money!" Tony O! said.

"And the first monkey I find hanging on the rims is going to have his ears cut off!" Mr. Thrush said. "I don't even think you guys should be able to use the gym if you're not in class."

"Anybody can use the gym?" Darnell asked.

"That's part of the deal," Mr. Thrush said. "It's going to be open at lunchtime."

"Then we won't have to play on those broken-down outdoor courts?" Tony O! said. "You can break your ankle on those outdoor courts because the blacktop is all messed up."

"They're going to be a parking lot," Mr. Thrush said.

"That's a good idea, too," Tony O! said, smiling. "Now I can bring my BMW to school."

"Yeah." Mr. Thrush picked up his briefcase and motioned toward the door. "Now get out of here."

"Hey, Mr. Thrush." Darnell, remembering the interview with Mr. Baker, decided to ask a good question this time. "What do you do when you're not in school?"

Mr. Thrush looked at Darnell. "None of your business! Now get outta here!"

FIVE

When Darnell got out of school there was only one bus in front. He didn't feel like riding. It was cool but not really cold, and he thought he would walk home. Tamika was on the bus, and ran to the front door as he passed.

"Why you walking?" Tamika asked.

" 'Cause I feel like it," Darnell said.

"You got any money?"

"If I had some I wouldn't give it to you," Darnell said.

"I'll clean your room for a week," Tamika said. "Honest."

Darnell handed over the quarter and got a pat on the cheek from his sister. Then she ran back into the bus.

The thing was, Tamika knew she could always get anything from Darnell that she wanted. Darnell knew it, too. Sometimes it made him mad, but when she asked him for anything he still found himself giving it to her.

Sometimes he liked walking through the streets of Oakdale. He often thought that if he were rich, really rich, he would travel to a lot of cities and just walk around by himself.

The school was thirty-four blocks from Darnell's house, and he had walked almost half the distance when he saw the men standing around the fire on Jackson Avenue.

Jackson Avenue was one of the oldest sections of Oakdale. There weren't any tall buildings on Jackson Avenue, just two-story houses, some of them containing stores. But half of the buildings were boarded up, and there were empty lots here and there. It was in one of the lots that Darnell saw the men standing around a fire they had built in an old oildrum. It wasn't that cold, and the four men were just standing and talking and looking at the fire.

"Hey! Young blood! Come over here!" one of the men called to Darnell.

Darnell stopped, and looked at the men.

"We ain't gonna bite you," the man said. "Come on over here. You scared?"

Darnell took a step closer to the men. "Scared of what?" he said, hoping his voice would stay low.

"I want you to run to the store for me," the man said. He was dark, darker than Darnell, and had a bushy beard. The beard was part white and part gray.

"What you want?" Darnell said. "I don't have time to go to no stores."

"Ain't you Sidney's boy?" the man said.

"Who are you?" Darnell asked.

"Sweeby Jones," the man answered, straightening his shoulders and standing taller. "Sweeby J. Jones."

"Sweeby?" Darnell smiled. "What kind of name is that?"

"When I was a kid my mother named me Robert, but my brother used to call me Sleepy because that's what I did all the time," Sweeby said. "But he couldn't say Sleepy, and I've been Sweeby every since."

"That's funny," Darnell said. "What you want from the store?"

"Two bottles of champagne and a quart jar of caviar!"

The four men started laughing and one of them slapped his hat against his leg.

"Make that four bottles of champagne!"

"He can't carry no four bottles of champagne," another man said. "Be reasonable!"

"You tell your father you saw me!" Sweeby Jones said.

"How you know my father?" Darnell asked, stepping closer.

"We were in the Army together," Sweeby said. "Viet—My Lovely—Nam."

"Where you work?" Darnell asked.

"How come he ask so many questions?" one of the other men asked. "He a doctor or something?"

"I ain't working, boy," Sweeby said. He looked away.

The four men looked at the fire. Now that he was closer, Darnell saw that one of the men was the same one he had seen in the supermarket. When he saw Darnell looking at him, he shifted his feet and squinted one eye. Darnell looked away. He didn't have to ask them to know they were probably home-less.

"Well, I got to go," Darnell said.

"Yeah, you go on along," Sweeby said. "You're a nice kid. I've seen you with your father. You look like a mannerly young boy to me."

"Some of these kids today don't know how to respect people," the man who had tried to steal the potato said.

" 'Bye."

Darnell walked down the street. He wanted to turn around and look at the men again, but he didn't. He couldn't wait to get home to talk to his father about Sweeby.

At home Darnell saw that Tamika had eaten some peanut butter and jelly sandwiches and left the open jars on the sink. He wanted to make a sandwich but he didn't want to put the jars back in when Tamika had left them out. He opened the refrigerator and found a banana and ate that.

He went into his bedroom, put on the television and his radio, and saw there was an envelope on his bed. In the envelope was a picture of him that Tamika had drawn. It wasn't bad, either. He opened his drawer and put it with the other pictures that Tamika had drawn of him.

He looked at his books, thought about starting his homework, and then began thinking about Sweeby Jones.

"Hey, Tamika!" he called out.

Tamika arrived at his door. "Speak, O turkey!"

"Dad home?"

"Yeah, but he went to the dentist," Tamika said. "You in trouble again?"

"No," Darnell said, a little annoyed that Tamika would say that he was in trouble. "But you know that guy that stole the potato?"

"Yeah?"

"I saw him in a lot over on Jackson Avenue," Darnell said. "And there was another guy there with him who was a friend of Dad's."

"What do I care?" Tamika asked.

"Later for you!"

"You like my picture?"

"Nope!"

Tamika went to Darnell's drawer to see if her picture had been placed with the others. She saw that it had been and smiled.

When his father came home his jaw was swollen and he went right to bed. Darnell would have to ask him about Sweeby another time. Maybe it was better, Darnell thought. He didn't want to talk in front of Tamika, and there was no way he could have a talk with his father without his sister listening if she was home.

"Stupid!" It was Wednesday afternoon, and Angie Cruz was screaming in the schoolyard. "I've never seen anything so stupid!"

There were a thousand kids running around the schoolyard at lunchtime, and Chris had told Jackson Holiday to pitch him a hardball. Jackson threw it underhand, and Chris hit it as hard as he could, and it went off his bat like a shot. It was a great shot except Chris was facing the school and the ball went right into the general office.

Everybody was screaming and getting out of the way of the falling glass, and Tony O! was there trying to figure out if the hit would have been a home run on the baseball field.

"This could be a big story," Tony O! was saying.

Mr. Baker stuck his head out another window, and a group of sixth-graders instantly pointed at Chris.

"I'll be right down!" he roared.

Some of the kids and two of the teachers cleared out of the yard as quickly as they could. By the time Mr. Baker reached the yard almost everyone had stopped what they were doing to look at him.

"Can you tell time, Mr. McKoy?" Mr. Baker's neck was swollen as he leaned over Chris.

"Yes, sir." Chris swallowed hard.

"Then at exactly eight-thirty tomorrow morning I expect to see your face in my office! Do you understand that?"

This time Chris's "Yes, sir" was so quiet the rest of the kids in the yard could hardly hear it.

Linda showed up with her notepad. Eddie Latimer was there, too, taking pictures of Mr. Baker dropping his attaché case.

"Get that camera out of here!" Mr. Baker yelled.

"I'm from the school newspaper!" Eddie said. He looked hurt that Mr. Baker had yelled at him.

Mr. Baker just stuffed his papers back into his attaché case and stalked across the yard to the parking lot.

"It was an accident," Chris was saying.

"Don't worry about it," Darnell said. "He'll probably just suspend you, have your mother come to school, and hang you by your thumbs for a little while."

"Man . . ."

That was Chris's way of saying that he knew he was in big trouble.

Miss Green came out the front door and made everybody go inside before they cut themselves on the glass.

Darnell went back into the school as soon as he could. You didn't mess with Mr. Baker when he got mad.

"Darnell." Miss Seldes called Darnell as he passed the library and asked if he had time to give her a hand. "Just a few minutes," she said.

Darnell didn't like Miss Seldes always talking to him like that. He liked her, but he didn't like a teacher being so friendly. It made him look a little bad, especially in front of the Corner Crew.

"What happened out there?" Miss Seldes asked.

"Chris hit a ball through a window," Darnell said. "It wasn't such a big thing, but all the sixth-graders are out there."

"And they're not nearly as mature as you seventh-graders, right?" Miss Seldes had that funny smile on her face that she got sometimes.

"That's right," Darnell said. "I'm more mature than I used to be a year ago."

"You probably are," Miss Seldes said. "Put the books on the cart according to the first number."

Darnell started to put the books on the cart, looking at the ones that were being borrowed. He knew that Miss Seldes was going to ask him some more questions. That's the way she was.

"The newspaper's going all right," Darnell said.

"You write any big stories yet?"

"I don't have any big stories to write," Darnell said. "I like sports and stuff like that, but Tony O! is the sports guy. I don't like the other stuff."

"What's the other stuff?"

"World peace," Darnell said. "Stuff like that. I mean, like, I want world peace, but I just don't want to write about it."

"Maybe you're more a human interest kind of writer," Miss Seldes said.

"What's that?"

"Well, you ever see somebody and wonder what they're all about?" Miss Seldes asked.

"Sort of." Darnell thought about Sweeby Jones.

"Perhaps you should write about people you want to know about," Miss Seldes said. "If you're interested in a person or persons, then other people might be interested in that person if you wrote about it."

"Could be," Darnell said. "Could be."

He had thought about not going to the meeting of the *Gazette* staff, but now he thought he would go and ask if he could just write about somebody who interested him.

The bell rang and he had to go to homeroom. Miss

Seldes asked him if he wanted to borrow a book and he said no.

The day dragged by slowly, and everything that could go wrong went wrong. Darnell had forgotten his math book, which they never used in class, and Mr. Ohrbach got angry.

"It's a good thing your head is screwed on," Mr. Ohrbach was saying, "or you would leave that home, too!"

Darnell didn't think it was funny. He had heard it a hundred times and the same people always laughed. He felt like getting up and walking out of math, but he knew that if one member of the Corner Crew got into trouble—and Chris was already in trouble for breaking the window—then the punishments would get worse and worse.

The *Gazette* staff meeting was supposed to start right after the final bell of the day, but Darnell had to copy the homework assignments from English and didn't get to the *Gazette* office until the fight between Kitty and Linda Gold had started. Linda was one of the most popular girls in the school and maybe the smartest. Darnell figured that if she quit the *Gazette* the paper would be in deep trouble. And from the way she looked he knew she meant it when she told Kitty that she didn't need to be on the paper.

"So quit," Kitty said. "If you don't need to be on the paper, then don't be on it!"

"You can't fire me," Linda said. "I'll quit when I'm good and ready!" She dropped three quarters in the soda machine.

"What's going on?" Mark asked.

"She wants to print this." Kitty pushed a sheet of paper across the desk. Mark read it aloud.

Mr. Baker, the principal of South Oakdale Middle School, left the school in the middle of a crisis when a window was shattered Thursday. When asked why he was leaving without finding out why the window had been broken, he appeared angry and refused to answer questions. He has still not answered the question as to whether his leaving was proper behavior for a school principal.

"Wait a minute." Jessica, who had been half listening to the conversation and half doing her math homework, looked up. "Everybody knows that Chris McKoy broke the window. Where was the crisis?"

"How did he know for sure it was Chris?" Linda said. "And how did he know it wasn't some gang or something who deliberately threw a ball through the window?"

"Maybe he asked somebody who saw it," Jennifer said.

"Then he should have told us," Linda said. "It would have taken only a minute or so."

"I don't think we should have that story in the paper," Mark said. "It's only going to get Mr. Baker madder."

"It won't be in the paper," Kitty said.

"That, my dear, is censorship," Linda said. "Is

that what the paper is about? Censorship? And can I write a story about censorship in middle schools?"

Kitty got up and started to walk out. Linda looked around the room and shrugged.

"Hey, Kitty, I got an idea for a story," Darnell said. He realized he was holding his breath.

"What is it?" Kitty said.

"It's about a guy I met on Jackson Avenue," Darnell said. "It's a human event story."

"Human interest," Mr. Derby said. He had been sitting in the back of the room looking through some quiz papers. "You've met someone you think you'd like to write about?"

"Yeah," Darnell answered.

"Who cares about him?" Kitty asked.

"Okay, so I won't write about him," Darnell said.

He picked up a copy of a magazine and started looking through it. He wasn't reading, not even looking at the pictures. He felt disappointed in himself.

"I didn't say you shouldn't write about him," Kitty said. "If you think it could be interesting, you should do it. Right, Mr. Derby?"

"I certainly think so," Mr. Derby said. "I'd be very much interested in who you think you should write about."

"You going to do it?" Mark asked.

"Maybe," Darnell said. "Maybe."

SIX

After school Darnell went home, changed his clothes, and started to do the English reading assignment while lying across his bed. Mrs. Finley had said that he should try to do the reading while he wasn't too tired. He knew she was right. Sometimes he would start reading something, then start daydreaming about what he was reading, and before he knew it he couldn't separate what he was reading from what he was daydreaming about. He read some more of *The Old Man and the Sea* and wondered why the author, some guy named Hemingway, had written about the old man. He knew that Chris wasn't right, that Hemingway thought the old man was a chump and just wanted to write about a chump.

Darnell had read the whole story once and hadn't figured it all out, and now he was reading it again, trying to remember what Mrs. Finley had said in class and what the other kids had said. He read for a while with the radio on, then started daydreaming about being on a boat with a big fish tied to the side of it. He couldn't figure how the old man could have caught the fish if he couldn't get it into the boat. It had to be some big fish. He imagined himself catching the fish, and then he imagined himself catching a shark, which was the biggest fish he knew about. But then he knew he would be afraid to try to tie it to the side of the boat. After a while he fell asleep.

When he woke he went to the kitchen, found some orange juice in the refrigerator, and poured a big glassful. No one was home. He looked out the front window and saw Larry on the stoop. He also saw some legs, which might have been Tamika's. Darnell had some more orange juice, went up to look for his keys, found them in the pockets of his school pants, and then went downstairs.

Tamika was sitting on the front stoop with Larry. They were drinking sodas. There was an old bike on the ground next to the stoop.

"Where did you get the sodas?" Darnell asked.

"The Black Muslims came by with a load of bean pies and sodas and I took the sodas from them," Tamika said. "I told them if they don't like it they can come and see you about it."

"Why you got to talk stupid all the time?" Darnell asked.

"No, man, that's true!" Larry said.

"Now she got you talking stupid, too," Darnell said. "You want to go over to the park and shoot some baskets?"

"No. Tamika said you and her can help me paint my bike."

"That's your bike?" Darnell asked, looking at the bike. It was all right looking, except that it was dirty and the spokes were rusty.

"Yeah, my dad got it for me," Larry said. "I got some spray paint."

"I told him what colors to get," Tamika said.

"How did you get spray paint?" Darnell said. He knew most stores wouldn't sell spray paints to anybody under eighteen.

"Them Black Muslims got it for me," Larry said, looking at Tamika and smiling.

"Yo, man, you still talking stupid, huh? Hey, I got it now," Darnell said, nodding his head. "You and Tamika got a thing going so you both talking stupid. That's love talk, right?"

"Get out of here!" Larry protested.

"You going to help him spray the bike?" Tamika asked.

"Yeah."

Darnell knew that Larry's parents were split and that he only saw his father once in a while. If his father bought him a bike, then it was more than he usually did. Larry mostly didn't like his father that much, so if he said anything good about him at all it was unusual.

Tamika got some newspapers and put them down, and then they laid the bike on the papers and started spraying it.

"You said you told Larry what colors to get?" Darnell asked his sister.

"Yeah."

"Well, he only got one color," Darnell said, holding up the two cans of navy blue spray paint.

"Well, that's all he needs," Tamika said. "This bike is going to look like Batman's motorcycle."

"No, it's not," Darnell said. "It's going to look like a bicycle painted blue."

"That's 'cause you can't paint," Larry said.

"Paint it yourself!" Darnell said. He put the paint can down and started up the stairs.

"Come on, give us a hand," Larry called to him.

"I got things to do," Darnell said.

"Come on, Darnell!" Larry called again.

When Larry and Darnell had an argument and Larry was sorry, he would always stretch out Darnell's name so that it sounded like Darn-Nell.

Darnell turned and pointed at his friend. "I'll see you later, Lar-Ree!" he said.

"Okay," Larry said. "See you later."

Darnell started up the long flights of winding stairs. When he got to his door he heard the phone ringing. He got in and grabbed the receiver. It was Benny Quiros.

"What's up?"

"You hear the news?" Benny asked.

"What news?"

"Linda went into the boys' locker room after the wrestling match," Benny said.

"Linda Gold?" Darnell asked.

"Yeah, she said she wanted to interview them," Benny said. "Only they were undressed when she went in, and she didn't even care."

"How come you calling me up to tell me that?" Darnell said.

"You're the only newspaper guy I know," Benny said.

SEVEN

"So, Dad, how do you feel?" Darnell sat on the end of the couch.

"What do you mean, how do I feel?" his father asked.

"You feel good?" Darnell asked. It was Saturday morning and his mother and Tamika had gone to their folk guitar class, leaving Darnell home with his father.

"I feel okay," his father answered. He moved the remote from one side of his lap to the other, away from where Darnell was sitting.

"So tell me," Darnell said. "How come you ended up with a place to stay and a family and everything and Sweeby ended up—you know—like he ended up."

"Sweeby? Sweeby Jones?"

"Yeah."

"Where you meet him?"

"Over on Jackson Avenue," Darnell said. "He looked like a homeless dude."

"Probably is!" his father said. Darnell saw his father's jaw tighten and relax.

"You mad because I saw him?"

"No." Mr. Rock's shoulders lifted and dropped. He turned toward Darnell, and there was the suggestion of a smile on his face. "Hey, he didn't say anything wrong to you, did he?"

"No."

"Well, I'm not mad at you for seeing him," his father said. "He told you he knew me?"

"Yeah. He said you and he were in Vietnam together."

"A hundred years ago," his father said quietly.

"A hundred years!"

"Not really a hundred years," his father said. "Just seems that way."

"How come you're okay and he's . . . like he is?" Darnell asked.

" 'Cause I took care of business," Mr. Rock said. "And he didn't. I come out the Army and looked for a job, took a few civil service tests, and got into the post office. Sweeby, he came out and talked some talk about getting into singing. I told him right then that singing wasn't nothing. Lots of people can sing but they ain't going nowhere."

"You ever hear him sing?"

"Yeah, I heard him plenty of times. Once we were in 'Nam, place called Cu Chi, and they had a little party. Nothing big, just something to get your mind off the war. An officer told him to go down into a hole and see if there was any Viet Congs down there. He got to the top of the hole and sang opera—that's what he sings—down into the hole. Damn Viet Cong came out and gave himself up."

"Get out of here!"

"That's the truth," Mr. Rock said.

"He sings opera?" Darnell asked.

"Yeah, but you can't just sing no opera. You got to study for ten, maybe fifteen years. Then you got to have a certain kind of voice. He should have taken the post office test."

"Is he smart?"

"Not smart enough to take the post office test," Mr. Rock said. He clicked the stations of the television, and Darnell watched as four stations in a row had commercials on.

"You don't think he could pass it?"

"He just didn't do the smart thing, like I did," Mr. Rock said. "You got to be smart, know what's going on in the world, so you can see what you need to do. I came out and saw there weren't any jobs around, so I took the test. That's why I'm where I am and he's where he's at."

"I'm thinking about interviewing him for the school newspaper," Darnell said.

"What for? You should interview some successful people so kids learn how to be successful," Mr. Rock said. "Anybody can learn how to be a failure."

"You ain't mad?" Darnell saw the little veins in his father's temple move.

"No," his father said. "Nothing to be mad about, is there?"

Darnell didn't want to say anything more. He knew his father was upset, but he couldn't figure out why. Maybe, he thought, his father had liked Sweeby and had wanted him to do better. Darnell watched television with his father, but images of Sweeby Jones standing on Jackson Avenue near the fire kept coming into his mind.

On Sunday, after church, Larry came over and told Darnell that the chain on his bicycle had broken. Darnell saw that he was disappointed.

"Maybe we can get a new one Monday from that place on Monticello that sells used bikes," Darnell said.

"Yeah, maybe," Larry answered.

Sometimes Darnell measured time by how much trouble he had during the day. It seemed that if he was having a bad day, time just dragged by, but if he was having a good day, it would go by fast. Monday morning started off as one of the slow days. Mr. Ohrbach gave a five-minute math quiz. Two of the problems were about square roots, and Darnell couldn't remember how to do them. He started the next one, which was one of those problems about two trains coming toward each other and you had to figure out how far they had traveled when they met. One was going at sixty miles an hour and the other one was going at seventy-five miles an hour. Darnell looked at the problem, tried figuring out how far the first train could go in fifteen minutes, decided that was wrong, and then heard Mr. Ohrbach say that the quiz was over.

"Great work, Darnell," Mr. Ohrbach said, shaking his head.

The test started the day off wrong, and nothing went particularly right after that. He had hoped for a good day because he wanted to try interviewing Sweeby that afternoon, and he didn't want to mess that up. But by three o'clock, after the test and forgetting his sneakers for gym, he was almost ready to forget the interview.

"Yo, Miss Seldes." Darnell saw Miss Seldes turning the lock in the library door with the key that hung around her neck.

"Hello, Darnell," Miss Seldes said. "The library is closed."

"Yeah, that's okay," Darnell said. "I just needed to ask you a question."

"I only have a minute," she said, already starting down the hall. "I have a meeting downtown this afternoon. What did you want?"

"If you interview somebody, what do you ask them?"

"You can ask them any questions you want," Miss Seldes said. "As long as you maintain their dignity. Put yourself in the place of the person you're going to interview. Imagine how it feels to be asked the questions you want to ask."

"Yeah, okay."

"Good luck with your interview," Miss Seldes said, pushing into the principal's office.

"Thanks," Darnell said, knowing that Miss Seldes couldn't have heard him. He went out the front door, stopping for a moment and shielding his eyes from the bright afternoon sun.

When his eyes had grown accustomed to the light, he looked over the schoolyard and finally spotted

Larry sitting with Mark Robbins. Larry said he had been looking for Darnell.

"How you looking for me when all you're doing is sitting here?" Darnell asked as they started off.

"I was waiting for you to come by," Larry said. "I thought we could get the chain for my bike."

"Okay, but I got some other stuff to do first," Darnell said.

Freddy Haskell waved as he went by. He was carrying a football.

"Let's see the ball!" Darnell called.

Freddy threw the ball. Darnell caught it and spun around as if he were the quarterback in a game. "Go deep!"

Freddy started running, zigzagging around imaginary opponents, and headed toward the school buses. Darnell threw a long, lazy spiral and watched Freddy run under it and catch it in stride.

"Man, he can catch a football!" Larry said.

"That's because I know how to throw one," Darnell said. "You got to put a spiral on it."

"He can still catch a ball," Larry insisted as they watched Freddy get on one of the buses. "What you have to do?"

"First we got to go to the supermarket and buy some pork and beans," Darnell said. "Then we're going to interview Sweeby Jones. He's that guy I saw on Jackson the other day."

"I'm not going to interview him!" Larry said.

"I got a tape recorder in my bag," Darnell said. "We'll give him the pork and beans, and then we'll ask him the questions."

"Why you going to give him pork and beans?"

" 'Cause he probably needs something to eat," Darnell said.

It was the first of the month, and the supermarket was crowded. They met Eddie Latimer, who was shopping for his grandfather, and then they saw Angelica Cruz.

"Hey, Angie!"

"Hi, Eddie," Angie replied. "Hi, Darnell, Larry."

"Angie's one of my fly girls," Eddie said.

"You wish!" Angie said.

"I'm trying to teach her how to kiss!" Eddie said. "But she won't take her glasses off and they get in the way."

"Eddie, why don't you grow up?" Angie said. "Either that or get back in your cage!"

"Oh, man, she really dissed you!" Larry said.

"That's 'cause we're in public," Eddie said. "If you guys weren't here she'd be throwing me one of them wet kisses."

"Eddie," Angie said, pushing past them, "do me a favor and die twice!"

Darnell found the pork and beans and said goodbye to Eddie. "I don't think you better mess with Angie," he said. "She can put you down in a minute."

"I think she really likes me," Eddie said.

"Yeah, especially if you do her a favor and die twice," Darnell said. "Later!"

When they paid for the beans Darnell saw that Angie was in another line but she wouldn't look toward them.

Jackson Avenue was bustling with people. A beer truck was double-parked on the street, and the traffic guard was arguing with the driver. Some older boys were standing on the corner, and Larry nodded at them.

"I think they're in a gang," he said to Darnell.

They went down Jackson, looking for Sweeby, and finally found him sitting on a milk crate outside a used-appliances store. There were two other men with him—a thin, brown-skinned man and an older man who was dark and had white stubble on his chin.

"We came to interview you," Darnell said. He held out the beans. "For the school newspaper."

"What's this?" Sweeby asked.

"Some beans," Darnell said.

"What you giving me this for?" There was a sharp edge to Sweeby's voice.

"Thought you might like some," Darnell said.

"I don't want your beans," Sweeby said.

"What he give you? A can of beans?" the oldest of the three men asked. "What he think he is, the Salvation Army?"

"Can I ask you some questions?" Darnell asked.

"No!" Sweeby said. "Get out of here!"

"I heard you could sing," Darnell said.

"Well, go back and ask your daddy the questions," Sweeby said, standing.

Darnell and Larry started down the street. Darnell looked back and saw that Sweeby was still standing, his hands jammed into his pockets.

"What you going to do now?" Larry asked. "Were you supposed to interview him for the paper?"

"No," Darnell said. "Just something I wanted to do."

They went to the used-bicycle shop, and the owner, a short, dark man with a big stomach, gave Larry a chain he said he had taken off an old bike.

"How much?" Larry asked.

"You have a choice," the man said. "One dollar or seventy-four dollars and thirty cents."

"I'll take the one dollar," Larry answered.

"How come I can't make any money in this business?" the man said.

When they reached Darnell's house, Tamika was in her room, and his mother said to leave her alone.

"What's wrong with her?" Darnell asked.

"Her friend is sick," his mother said. "You know Molly Matera?"

"She's always sick," Larry said.

"Well, she's sick again." Darnell's mother looked into the bag that Darnell had put on the table. "Your father told you to buy that?"

"No, he bought it to give it to a homeless dude, but the homeless dude said he didn't want it," Larry said.

"Shut up, Larry!"

"You did that?" his mother asked. "That was nice of you."

"Yeah, but the guy didn't take it," Larry said.

"Shut up, Larry."

"You going to help me paint the bike?" Larry asked.

The bike already looked good, painted a glistening dark blue, almost black. They put another coat of paint on the handlebars and on the spokes.

"Now all it needs is my name on the side," Larry said.

"Why don't you wait until tomorrow," Darnell said. "Then let Tamika put your name on the side."

"What she doing now?"

"You heard my mom say not to mess with her," Darnell said.

"I can't wait until tomorrow," Larry said.

"Then mess it up now," Darnell said. "You know you going to mess it up because you can't paint as good as Tamika."

"Yeah," Larry said. "Okay, you ask her if she'll do it right after school tomorrow. Okay?"

"Okay."

When Larry left, Darnell did his homework, and then he wrote down what happened when he talked to Sweeby. When he had finished he looked at what he had written. Then he thought about what Miss Seldes had said about putting himself in the place of the person he wanted to interview. It wasn't the questions that had bothered Sweeby, it was the can of pork and beans.

Darnell looked at what he had written, tore it up, and then started writing again.

In the morning they had some firemen come into the school and talk about safety in the home. Four classes at a time went into the library. Darnell had already given his story to Kitty. She hadn't read it, just put it in her notebook and smiled at him. He had a feeling that she liked him. Anyway, she was always smiling at him. Darnell was thinking about her when he heard Angie's voice from the back of the library.

"Oh, Eddie," she called out, "what's that on your nose?"

Everybody turned around to look at Eddie Latimer. He had his head down, but you could see that he had the biggest zit on his nose that Darnell had ever seen.

"Nothing!" Eddie said.

"Nothing?" Angie called out. "It's so big and red I thought it was a traffic light!"

Darnell made a mental note never to get in an argument with Angie Cruz.

"Why don't you shut up!" Eddie said.

"If you had it pierced you could wear an earring in it," Angie said.

Some of the kids started laughing, and Eddie sat down and put his hand over his face. It was good he had big hands.

"You could be growing a new nose," Angie said.

The fire department guys seemed really cool. They were all young, and two of them had actually gone to South Oakdale when it had been a high school. But they talked about smoke detectors, and they talked about them in a boring way. Even the way their voices sounded was boring, and most of the kids started looking out of the window or passing notes to each other.

"Can I ask everybody here one question?" one of

the firemen asked. "How many people here think smoke detectors are boring? Raise your hands."

A few hands went up.

"Be honest," he said. "How many of you think this whole talk was a little boring?"

Most of the hands went up.

"That's the problem," the young fireman said. "Most people think the subject is boring, and it is. But when you have a fire in your home, and it catches you by surprise, it's really exciting! And when somebody gets hurt, or somebody dies, then that's exciting, too. And all because smoke detectors are . . . what?"

Somebody said "boring."

"How many kids are not too bored to go home and check their smoke detectors today?"

All the hands went up.

On the way out of the library Miss Seldes stopped Darnell and asked how the interview went.

"Not too good," he said. "He told me to go away."

"Your mistake or his?"

"Mine," Darnell said.

"Then you'll be better the next time," she said. She had a pleased look on her face.

The day went slowly. Darnell got his math test back and found that he had failed it. He had gotten 50 out of a possible 100. Tamika got 70.

"That's 'cause I'm smarter than you," Tamika said when she saw him after class.

"What's wrong with Molly Matera?" Darnell asked.

Tamika turned and walked quickly away.

It wasn't until the last period of the day that word reached Darnell. There was a note on all the bulletin boards in the school that if anyone wanted to answer his editorial they had to do it before the end of the week.

"What editorial?" Darnell asked Mark.

"The one that's on the bulletin board," Mark said. "I thought it was pretty good."

Darnell went into the hall, and went to the bulletin board. There was the notice from Kitty.

If anyone wishes to write a reply to the editorial that appears below and will be in the next issue of the *South Oakdale Gazette*, please have the reply *neatly typed* and in the *Gazette* office by Friday.

—Kitty Gates, editor in chief

Under Kitty's note was what he had written the night before.

Everybody is talking about how to help the homeless and how to solve the problems that our society is facing. The homeless don't want to just be given things, they want to have dignity and to help themselves. Instead of turning the old basketball courts into a parking lot and messing up the environment even more by having more cars on the road, why not turn it into a garden where the homeless

people could raise vegetables that they
could eat? That way they could help
themselves and we would make better use
of the courts.

                              —Darnell Rock

"That's a dumb idea, Darnell." Linda Gold was
looking over Darnell's shoulder.
"I don't think so," Darnell said.
Linda just shook her head and walked away.

For the rest of the day Darnell was excited. At least a
dozen kids came up to him to talk about the article
on the bulletin board. He felt proud of it, in a way,
and scared, too. It was the first time he had had so
much attention.
Darnell didn't see Tamika until he got home.
"Hey, you see my article on the bulletin board?"
he asked.
"Yeah," Tamika said. "It was nice."
"How you feeling?" Darnell could see that Tamika
wasn't doing too well.
"Okay."
"You hear from Molly?"
"I spoke to her this morning before I came to
school," Tamika said. "She's got a problem with her
kidneys or something."
"She coming back to school?"
"She thinks so," Tamika said. "I sure hope she's
going to be okay. It's scary having someone so sick
they could die or something."
"She could die?"

Tamika nodded.

Darnell went into his room, put his radio on, then turned it off and looked at his homework. He thought about starting it and getting it all done, extra neatly. He knew he could surprise everyone if he did. He looked at the math first. Triangles. He had never liked triangles. Even when the teacher talked about how triangles were so important in the building of the pyramids, he hadn't liked them. He closed his math book and told himself that he would do the homework later. Then he opened it again and told himself that he knew he wouldn't really do it later. Then he closed it again, and said that maybe he would.

When he heard his father come in, he went out to see him.

"Hi!" Darnell slid into the overstuffed chair near the window.

"Humm!" his father grunted.

"I got an idea," Darnell said. "What you think about having homeless people grow their own food?"

"They won't even walk to the supermarket for their own food," his father said. "How they going to grow it? That's hard work, man."

"Oh," Darnell said.

His father turned on the television, clicked through a few channels, and settled on a program in which cops were making a drug arrest.

Darnell thought about the article on the bulletin board and wondered if he should mention it to his father again. There was still that thing going on, his father's being a little mad when Darnell talked about Sweeby or homeless people.

When Darnell got to school the next day, Mr. Ohrbach, the math teacher, was putting up a poster on the bulletin board about scholarships.

"We're not even in high school yet," Darnell said to him. "We can't get scholarships."

"That's right," Mr. Ohrbach said, stapling the top of the notice to the board. "But you can get an idea of what they give scholarships for."

Darnell looked at the notice and saw that it was a scholarship for math and science students. That figured, with him being the math teacher.

During the lunch period an announcement was made that all the band members had to make sure they had their permission slips if they were going to the tristate music festival. Benny Quiros and Colin Rigby started their imitation of a jazz band, and both of them were kicked out of the cafeteria. Then Freddie Haskell, who played trombone in the band, said that Benny and Colin were immature. Chris McKoy went out into the hallway and told Benny and Colin. Then Colin came back into the cafeteria and punched Freddy. This was more or less the way that Colin got suspended for a day, which was the first time in almost a year that anyone outside of the Corner Crew had been suspended.

EIGHT

"Hey, you're in the *Journal*!" Tamika knocked over the container of milk on the table, sending a stream of the white liquid toward her father.

"What?" Her father jumped up, knocking his chair over backward.

Mrs. Rock grabbed the milk container with her right hand and wiped most of the milk up with one swipe of the dishrag in the other.

"I'm in the paper?" Mr. Rock asked.

"No, Darnell is," Tamika said, spreading a copy of the *Oakdale Journal* on the table. "Listen to this: 'Mrs. Estelle Joyner spoke at the City Council meeting last night, asking them to continue their plans for building a parking lot at South Oakdale. She said she had heard that they had seen an editorial in the school newspaper that had influenced them. The editorial was written by Darnell Rock, a seventh-grader. The Council put off a decision on the parking lot until the next meeting.' "

"You were down to the City Council meeting?" Mr. Rock was picking up the chair.

"No," Darnell answered. "I don't even know what it is."

"It's where the city does its business," Mrs. Rock said. "They pass laws, decide on what taxes they're going to have, and determine how the city is going to spend its money."

"Somebody must have sent them your article," Tamika said.

"You're going to find out when you get to school," Mrs. Rock said. "I'm anxious to find out myself. This is the first time anybody in the family has been in the paper."

"I was in the paper," Mr. Rock said. "When I went into the Army they had me in a list of all the guys that went in from our neighborhood."

"Sweeby, too?" Darnell asked.

"I guess so," his father answered gruffly.

"You guys better get out of here before you're late." Mrs. Rock took the bowl of cereal from in front of Tamika.

"I'm not finished," Tamika said.

"Yes, you are," Mrs. Rock said as the phone rang.

"I bet that's somebody who read about you in the paper," Tamika said.

She beat her mother to the phone and answered it. All eyes were on her as she answered. She shook her head twice, then said that she would "see if he is in." All the time she was pointing to Darnell and at the newspaper.

"It's somebody from the newspaper!" she whispered as loudly as she could as she handed the receiver to her brother.

Darnell felt a sick feeling in the pit of his stomach. He didn't want to talk to anybody from the newspaper.

"Hello?"

"Darnell Rock?"

"Yeah?" Darnell looked at his mother. She was drying a dish and looking at him with wide eyes.

"My name is Peter Miller, and I'm going to be at South Oakdale this afternoon to interview the principal—I think his name is Mr. Baker—about the parking lot thing. I wonder if you'd be available at lunchtime?"

"Yeah," Darnell said, "I guess so. But I don't know how the City Council got my article."

"Some mother saw it when she came to school to bring her kid's flute for band practice," Peter Miller said. "Her husband's on the City Council, and she gave it to him. Anyway, I'll look for you at twelve. Okay?"

"Yeah, okay."

At school everybody had either read the article in the *Journal* or had heard about it. Two kids he didn't even know waved copies at him, and a sixth-grader asked him for his autograph. Most of the kids were saying that turning the parking lot into a garden to feed the homeless was a good idea.

"It's a cute idea, Darnell," Mrs. Joyner said, stopping him in the hallway. "But do you know anything about raising vegetables?"

"No," Darnell said with a shrug.

"And do you think the vagrants around the school

70

will?'' she asked, turning sharply on her heel before he had a chance to answer. He watched her walk quickly down the hall.

Estelle Joyner was one of the best-looking teachers in the school. She taught music and commercial skills and was a homeroom teacher, too. Darnell didn't know why she was against the garden.

"She probably just wants a place to park her car," Larry said at recess.

"What kind of car she drive?" Darnell asked.

"She got a bad Vo!" Larry said, referring to the silver Volvo that Miss Joyner had recently bought. "She got black-tinted windows and everything."

"I should tell her if she let me drive it I'll say they should make the courts into a parking lot," Darnell said.

"She ain't gonna let you drive it because she's stuck up," Larry said. "She thinks she cute."

"She is cute," Darnell said.

"You really care about if they make it a garden or not?" Larry asked.

"I don't know," Darnell said. "It's an idea. You know, maybe it would be cool. I think it's better than a parking lot. I don't know nothing about raising vegetables or stuff like that, though."

"You didn't know nothing about writing for a newspaper until you did it," Larry said. "Yo, there goes Freddy. You want to mess with him?"

"Yeah." They walked over to where Freddy Haskell was talking to Paula. Freddy's back was against the wall, and Darnell just stood as close to him as he could. He didn't speak at all.

71

"Hi," Freddy said, trying to back away.

"Hi?" Darnell looked at Freddy. "Who told you you could speak to a seventh-grader?"

"You came over here," Freddy said.

"What's that supposed to mean?" Darnell found himself starting to laugh and looked away. "You messing with me?"

"No," Freddy said, smiling.

"Hey, look." Larry pointed at Freddy. "He's laughing at you. Don't hit him, Darnell! Don't hit him!"

Larry grabbed Darnell as if he were preventing a fight and yelled at Freddy to run. Freddy took a look at Darnell, couldn't figure out whether he was really mad or not, and then ran down the hall.

"Get out of the hallway!" Mr. Baker's voice boomed as he spoke. "And, Darnell, get into the office and wait for me there!"

"Man, I wasn't doing nothing!" Darnell complained.

"You weren't doing *anything*," Mr. Baker corrected Darnell's English. "And you had better be in the office when I get there. You, too, Larry."

Darnell could feel himself getting mad. He didn't like being in trouble, and he especially didn't like it today, when everybody was talking about him. He was doing okay, and now Mr. Baker was just putting him down. He sat on the end of the bench and didn't even answer Larry when he spoke to him.

Mark Robbins came into the office to leave some papers with the school secretary. When he saw

Darnell sitting in the office, he asked what had happened.

"Mind your business," Darnell said, "before I bust you in your face!"

"You know"—Mark sniffed as he spoke—"I know karate."

He gave Darnell what he imagined was a tough look as he left the office.

Guys like Mark never got into trouble, Darnell thought. Chris McKoy said that they didn't get into trouble because they were white, but that wasn't right, Darnell thought. Guys like Mark were always doing the right thing, always doing the homework, always being on time. And after a while people just expected them to be all right, the same way that people expected him to be doing something wrong.

The clock on the wall moved slowly, and the period was half over before Mr. Baker came back into the office. He glanced at Darnell and Larry and told them both to sit up.

"What is the matter with you boys?" Mr. Baker asked angrily.

"Nothing," Larry said.

Darnell looked over at Larry and saw that he was looking away from Mr. Baker toward the globe on top of a file cabinet.

"School is not a game you're here to play," Mr. Baker said. "One day you're both going to learn that the hard way. Now get on back to your classes!"

Larry waited until they got out into the hallway to call Mr. Baker a turkey. "We weren't even doing nothing," he said.

"We weren't doing *anything*!" Darnell said.

There was a basketball game between boys and girls at lunchtime, and Tony O!, Eddie, and Darnell were playing against Tamika, Kitty Gates, and a Puerto Rican girl named Nicholasa. Nicholasa was the best artist in the school.

"Tamika, hit Eddie on his zit!" Angie called out. "You can't miss it."

"Shut up!" Eddie called.

Darnell knew that the girls would be easy to beat if the boys played as hard as they could. But when they played against girls, they had to beat them while they were looking cool, which was kind of hard to do, especially with Tamika playing.

Tamika could play any sport, she was just that good. Kitty wasn't as good as Tamika, but she tried like anything and she hated to lose. Darnell passed the ball a lot, giving it over to Tony O! and Eddie. The game went to 10, and it was Nicholasa who scored the final points as the girls won, 10 to 6.

"It was your fault, man," Tony O! said, pointing at Eddie. "You didn't score a point."

"I'll score a point on your head!" Eddie said. "You should have been playing with the girls. You look like one!"

"Hey, Darnell!" Donald Williams had a high, squeaky voice. "This guy is looking for you. He's from the newspaper!"

Everybody turned to see Peter Miller. He was tall and had a full, light brown beard. He reached out and shook Darnell's hand.

"Can we go someplace and talk?" he asked. "Somewhere we can hear each other?"

"We can go in the library," Darnell said.

Darnell tried not to notice the other kids looking at him as he and Peter Miller walked off the basketball courts toward the school.

"Are these the courts that are going to be torn down?" the reporter asked.

"Yes, sir," Darnell said.

"Call me Peter," the reporter said. "When did you first get the idea for making this a garden for the homeless?"

"I met this guy," Darnell said. "He's homeless and everything. I always see him, you know, on Jackson Avenue. You know where Jackson Avenue is?"

"Sure. It's a beat-up neighborhood, a real ghetto," Peter said.

Darnell looked at Peter. "What's that mean?" he asked.

"It's . . . just not a nice part of town," Miller said.

They reached the library, and Miss Seldes nodded toward them. Darnell was glad to see her in the library. They found a seat in the corner, and Darnell sat facing the window.

"So how would this garden work?" Peter asked.

"I don't know too much about gardens," Darnell said. "But I guess they could grow vegetables and stuff there."

"You think they could grow enough to keep from being hungry?"

Darnell thought of Sweeby, and of the man who

had stolen a potato. Then, for the first time, he felt ashamed of himself. Here he was talking about feeding the homeless and he didn't know anything about it at all. He thought of just getting up and walking away, or telling Peter that maybe he was wrong.

"Maybe you can't feed all the people that's hungry," he said. "But you could give them a chance to help out and feed themselves. They feel better when they can help themselves."

"You really think they want to help themselves?"

"Yeah."

"How do you know?"

"I'm interviewing one of the guys now," Darnell said. "Not right now, not this minute, but I've been talking to him for a while. And I know he wants to help himself. You know, you got to let people have their dignity, and stuff."

"Oh, yeah." Peter looked at Darnell. "You think you could get this guy to talk to me? Might make a good human interest story."

"I guess so," Darnell said.

Peter went over to Miss Seldes and spoke to her. Darnell saw her nod, and then Peter beckoned for Darnell to come over to where he stood near the phone.

Peter dialed and then asked for a Mickey Anderson. Susan Seldes was looking at some file cards, but Darnell thought she just wanted to listen.

"Hello? Mr. Anderson?" Peter made a circle with his thumb and forefinger and nodded toward Darnell. "Hello, I'm over at South Oakdale. I'm talking to the kid who wrote the article on making the

basketball courts into a garden for . . . right . . .
right. . . . Anyway, he says he's going to interview
a homeless guy. I was thinking that maybe I should
do it for the paper. Might make a good human interest . . . what? What? He's only a kid. . . . Yeah,
just a minute."

Peter's expression changed as his mouth tightened. He looked over at Darnell.

"You don't think you could do the interview for
the *Journal*, do you?" Peter Miller was shaking his
head from side to side, signaling "no."

Behind him Miss Seldes was nodding her head up
and down.

"Yeah," Darnell said. "I can do it."

Darnell absolutely knew that the two hardest people
in the school to talk to were Angie Cruz and Tony O!
Talking to Tony O! was like being a traffic cop in a
Roadrunner cartoon. You had to hold him down to
get two sensible words out of him. And Angie talked
a mile a minute. She talked so fast she would be on
the next sentence while you were still trying to figure out what she said in the last one. So when he
saw Angie and Tony O! arguing in front of the building, he stopped to listen. Angie was doing most of
the talking, while Tony O! was playing an imaginary
game of basketball around her.

"I can't even figure out why Johnny wants to be on
the track team if he can't run fast," Angie was saying.

"Lots of people want to be on a team." Tony O!
stopped his imaginary dribble to catch his breath.

"It's cool to be on a basketball team or a track team. You get to wear a uniform, and you get to hang out with the team. That's all cool stuff."

"Yeah, could be," Angie said. "But it doesn't make a lot of sense if you can't run fast."

"So, maybe he thinks he can run fast," Tony O! answered.

"You said he can't," she said.

"I know he can't," Tony O! said. "I've seen him running. He can't beat anybody."

Tony O! jiggled and wiggled around for a little while and then bumped Angie with his hip and went up for an imaginary shot.

"Is running fast something you can learn how to do?" she asked, looking toward Darnell.

"I don't think so," Tony O! said. "You have to be born fast, like me."

"So why is Chris McKoy telling him he can be on the team?" Angie said.

"How do I know?" Tony O! said.

"What's happening?" Darnell came over and asked. Angie looked away for a moment, then turned back toward Darnell and smiled.

"Did I ever mention to you that everybody in the Corner Crew, especially Chris McKoy, stunk?" Angie said.

"Yo, what did the reporter want?" Tony O! asked.

"Yo yourself, budgie-brain!" Angie snapped. "Don't you see I'm talking to Darnell?"

"What did Chris do?" Darnell asked.

"I think he's convinced my brother to try out for

the track team," Angie said. "All he's going to do is lose."

"So that's not terrible," Darnell said.

"I guess not," Angie said, "if you're a loser!"

The two boys watched as Angie stalked off, trying to adjust her book bag over one shoulder.

"Hey, man." Tony O! shook his head. "She got pissed and you got dissed!"

"The way it be sometimes," Darnell said with a shrug.

"So what did the reporter want?"

"The *Journal* might publish my interview with a homeless guy," Darnell said.

"Word?"

"Word!" Darnell said. "You can ask Miss Seldes."

"Man, that's fresh!"

"What can I tell you?" Darnell said. "You see Larry around?"

"No," Tony O! said. "You know, if you do an interview you should put it in the school paper first."

"Yeah, I guess," Darnell said.

Darnell looked for Larry, couldn't find him, and went to the first class of the afternoon, one he had with Tamika. He was wondering if he should ask Tamika to go with him to interview Sweeby. Tamika wouldn't take no for an answer even if Sweeby didn't want to talk. But she had a fast mouth and might get everybody mad. Larry wouldn't say anything, but he would go with him and be on his side.

Nicholasa and Tamika were sitting in the back of the room, and Tamika was braiding Nicholasa's hair while the teacher was reading some poetry.

"Tamika, what are you doing?" Mrs. Finley asked.

"I'm following the mood of the poetry," Tamika said. "That kind of poetry makes me want to do somebody's hair."

"Haiku makes you want to do somebody's hair?" Mrs. Finley screwed up her face in disbelief.

"Yeah," Tamika answered. "Ain't it strange?"

"Leave her hair alone and concentrate on trying to get the feel of the poetry!" Mrs. Finley was turning red.

"But if her hair isn't right she's going to get upset," Tamika said. "I think she's upset now. Nicholasa, baby, are you upset?"

"I don't think so," Nicholasa said in a quiet voice.

"Does any of you know what the purpose of education is?" Mrs. Finley asked. "Does anybody here know?"

Tamika raised her hand, and Mrs. Finley gave her a look that lowered it.

Darnell was nervous the whole afternoon. Even when the dog got into the school and ran into the girls' bathroom, he couldn't keep his mind off the interview. He thought to himself that Sweeby might not even be on Jackson Avenue. He had never seen him anyplace else, but it was possible, he thought.

By the time the final bell rang, he had decided to postpone the interview for at least another day.

"Hey, Angie, your brother's in a fight!"

Darnell didn't hear who said it, but he saw a crowd of kids looking out the window. He went over to look and saw that Angie's brother, Johnny, was standing near the fence in the yard and Benny and Larry were standing in front of him. Chris looked as if he was pushing him.

Darnell went out the front door and down the side steps. He had to go all the way around the small toolshed to get to the yard. When he got into the yard he went up to where Johnny was still against the fence with Benny in his face.

"You want to be on the track team, you got to practice!" Benny was yelling. "And you got to do it all the time or else you're not going to be on the team!"

"Leave him alone!" Angie was there, and she pushed Benny. He pushed her back, hard.

"So what are you going to do?" Benny Quiros was yelling again.

"Leave him alone!" Angie was screaming at Benny. She pushed past Benny and grabbed her brother's arm. "Come on."

"No," he said, pushing her hand away from him.

"Johnny, come on!" she called to him.

"No," he said, pushing past her and heading toward the track. "I got to practice."

"What are you doing?" she called after him.

"Leave him alone." Darnell spoke softly to Angie. "Hey, Angie, don't worry, he'll be okay."

Angie walked away stiffly, tears running down her face. She was worried about her brother. Darnell watched her for a long moment, thinking about how concerned she looked, thinking about her brother, thinking about how some of the people from the Corner Crew were doing some really good things. Then his thoughts went from the Corner Crew to the guys standing around the fire on Jackson Avenue.

NINE

Larry was at Darnell's house on Saturday morning and was watching television in the kitchen with Tamika when Darnell finished dressing. They were having cookies and milk.

"Larry's got a milk mustache," Tamika said.

"Why don't you kiss it off for him," Darnell said.

"What is your problem, Darnell?" Tamika threw a towel at her brother.

"Larry, you ready?" Darnell asked his friend.

"Just because you're in a hurry to interview that homeless dude don't mean that Larry has to be," Tamika cut in.

"Suppose he's not there," Larry said, putting cookies in his pocket.

"Then he's not there," Darnell said. "He was there the last time."

"How come Benny and everybody is going to coach Angie's brother in track?" Tamika asked.

"So he can beat you," Darnell said, grabbing his pad and pen off the counter. "I'm going."

"Wait up!" Larry called.

Darnell hit the street and felt the cool wind in his

face. He had heard earlier that it might rain, and he looked up at the late morning sky. There were clouds in the distance, but they were light, almost fluffy against the graying sky. On the apartment building across from where he lived, a flock of pigeons was being rousted from their coop by a thin man wearing dark shorts and a brown T-shirt.

"That's Benny's father," Larry said.

"What do you think I should ask him?" Darnell walked near the edge of the sidewalk.

"Ask him why he keeps so many pigeons on the roof," Larry said.

"Not him!" Darnell shot a glance at Larry, saw that he still had a smidgen of the milk mustache, and smiled. "I mean Sweeby."

"You better say something nice," Larry said. "My mom said you better not mess with homeless people because they ain't got nothing to lose."

Darnell was quiet the rest of the way over to Jackson Avenue. He kept going over questions in his mind, but none of them sounded right.

There were usually a few people, mostly women, on Fairview Street where Darnell lived. But as he walked toward Jackson Avenue, there were more and more people on the street. Darnell knew that there would be even more people on Jackson Avenue.

"You know whose idea it was to coach Johnny Cruz?" Larry asked.

"Whose?" Darnell buttoned his jacket.

"Sonia's," Larry said. "She saw some guys from

the eighth grade cracking on him and she caught an attitude."

"She's always got an attitude," Darnell said. "But usually she's right. Anyway, I'd like to see if we can get him to run fast."

"We ought to get Tamika to coach him," Larry said. "She can aggravate you so much you'll want to run fast just to shut her mouth."

"You going to marry Tamika," Darnell said. "You always talking about her."

"Hey, look." Larry nodded with his head. "I bet you that's not a real store."

They had turned onto Jackson Avenue from Ege Street. Darnell saw bags of onions piled on a wooden box in front of the window. The sign on the window that read MACK'S GROCERYS barely covered the old sign that read LA CARNICERÍA FAMOSA.

"Let's get on down the street," Darnell said.

"You scared to look in there?" Larry asked. "I'll go on in."

Darnell stopped and leaned against a utility pole. "Go on in, man," he said. "I'll wait for you."

Larry smiled and kept walking. Darnell caught up with him and punched him on the arm.

Sweeby was standing in front of Ace's Barbershop. Darnell and Larry reached him just as a light rain began to fall.

"Excuse me, Mr. Sweeby." Darnell waved his hand in greeting. "I'd like to have another chance to interview you."

"Read about your little narrow butt in the paper," Sweeby said. "Think you a big deal, huh?"

"No," Darnell said with a shrug.

"What you want to ask me?" Sweeby said. "And how much you going to pay me for an interview?"

"Pay you?" Darnell looked over at Larry and saw that Larry was looking at Sweeby. "I ain't got no money."

"You ain't giving out no free cans of beans?"

"Naw."

"Okay," Sweeby said. He turned and looked in the barbershop. "Come on in here."

Ace's Barbershop was one of the best places to go on a Saturday morning. That was when the men who were waiting to get their hair cut sat inside and talked man talk with Ace and Preacher, the two barbers. Preacher was bald but wore a big, curly wig. Ace was big with a rough, gravelly voice. What they talked about was just about anything. Sometimes they talked about how the city was being run, and sometimes they talked about what the Arabs or the French people were doing. A lot of the time they just talked about what was going on in the neighborhood.

"Preacher, you mind if this boy interviews me here?" Sweeby asked Preacher. Ace wasn't there. "He's that kid that said they should turn the basketball court into a garden for the homeless."

"Who's your daddy?" Preacher asked.

"Sidney Rock," Darnell said. "He works for the post office."

"Yeah, I know him," Preacher said in a flat voice. "Go on, do your interview."

"I'm going to tape the interview, okay?" Darnell asked.

"Yeah, go on," Sweeby said. He straightened up and squared his shoulders.

Larry sat down as Darnell set up his tape recorder. A man who was sitting in one of the chairs reading a paper folded it and put it down. He crossed his legs and turned toward Darnell and Sweeby. Darnell felt a lump in the middle of his stomach.

"So, where were you born?" Darnell asked.

"I was born in Live Oak, Florida," Sweeby said, "in the year nineteen hundred and forty-three."

"Then what happened?" Darnell asked.

"*Then what happened?'!*" Preacher stopped clipping hair. "You want the man to give you his whole life after he was born? You got to ask him some questions!"

"You have a job?" Darnell asked, wishing Preacher had kept his mouth shut.

"Had all kinds of jobs," Sweeby said. "Good jobs, too. Worked up in Kentucky for a while as a driller in a mine, worked in New York City down on the docks, worked in Jersey City for Western Electric. That was a sweet job."

"Till they closed," Preacher said.

"I know whole families used to work for them," the man who had been reading the paper said.

"So how come you . . . you know . . . you don't have a job now?" Darnell asked.

"Why you think I don't have a job?" Sweeby said.

Darnell looked at Larry, then at Preacher. "You don't dress so hot," he said finally.

"Did I tell you that you don't dress so hot yourself?" Sweeby said. "You got a job?"

"No."

"But you got somebody to take care of you, right?"

"Sure."

"Well, Sweeby Jones don't have nobody to take care of him," Sweeby said. "And the little piece of job I got don't pay nobody's rent today. When I was a young man I used to get a job here or there and I could keep a roof over my head. Today, if you don't have a woman or some kind of partner, you got to make big money to keep an apartment."

"So how come you don't have a good job?" Darnell asked.

Sweeby took off his hat and turned his head from side to side. "You see these ears of mine?"

Darnell looked at them. They were small, like Larry's. "I see them."

"Well, I ain't got a good job because I ain't got nothing between these ears that anybody is going to pay any good money for."

"You know what I always say"—Preacher was giving a guy in the chair a nice fade—"it's a good thing your stomach don't control your feet. Because you know that if your stomach controlled your feet it would be kicking you in the hind parts every time it got hungry for all the dumb things you did in your life."

"What dumb things did you do?" Darnell asked.

"Did what folks expected me to," Sweeby said. "They expected me to sit in the back of the room like a big dummy, and that's what I did. Then they expected me to get out of school with nothing but a strong back, and I did that."

"That's what they expected all of us to do," Preacher said. "And it didn't make much difference if you knew something or not, unless you were a preacher or a teacher."

"Or an undertaker," the customer waiting said. " 'Cause you know down South the white undertakers didn't take no colored business."

"You never got your high-school diploma?" Larry asked.

"Hey, who's this?" Preacher asked. "He your coanchor person?"

"He's my friend," Darnell said.

"You think they don't have any high schools in Live Oak?" Sweeby said. "Sure they got high schools, and sure I got my diploma. But when you got a piece of paper in your hands it don't mean that you got something between your ears."

"When I was a young man . . ." Preacher stopped cutting hair and put his scissors down.

"I'm going to be an old man if you don't finish cutting my hair," his customer said.

"You free to go anytime you want," Preacher said. "You can just pay me for half a haircut."

The customer gave Darnell a dirty look.

"When I was a young man you could always get a job if you were willing to work, and just about any old job would see you through. Didn't mean you ate high on the hog, but you ate. Now if you don't have a decent job you can't make it for nothing. You could just be strong then and make a living. Lifting and carrying and stuff like that."

"You could dig a ditch," Sweeby said. "You remember when they laid that cable under Jackson Avenue?"

"Yeah, and colored folks were the last ones to get their homes wired up," Preacher said.

"They must have had a hundred men digging for three weeks steady," Sweeby went on. "Today they get two men with a back hoe and dig up from here to Bayonne in four days."

"So what you going to do?" Darnell asked.

"Try to eat enough to keep my body and soul together," Sweeby said. "Then hope I can sneak up on some learning so I can make a decent living."

"Can you read?" Darnell asked.

"Didn't I just tell you I read about you in the paper?"

"Then how come you can't get a good job?" Darnell asked.

"Can you read?" Preacher asked. "And are you working?"

"He ain't nothing but a kid," Larry said.

"Well, kid, ask your coanchor over there what difference it makes if you're a kid or not. If you can't do nothing the man is going to pay for, then you're in a world of trouble."

Darnell looked out the barbershop window. Across the street, two young men leaning against a fence were talking to a girl holding a baby. The light rain had already stopped.

"So what are you going to do?" Darnell asked.

"You already asked that question," the waiting customer said.

"If I knew what to do to get myself straight, I would go out and do it," Sweeby said. "You can sit in your house and think about what it's like out here in the street, but unless you out here, you don't know. You just don't know."

"What you think about the garden idea?" Darnell asked.

"It's something," Sweeby said. "It's not a great idea, but it's something. You letting people know we here. People want to forget that poor people exist. We ain't pleasant."

"Are you homeless?" Darnell asked.

"Homeless?" Sweeby leaned back as far as he could and looked at Darnell. "No, I'm not homeless. I sleep in these buildings right here on Jackson Avenue. They're my home. Or I go over to St. Lucy's and sleep, and then that's my home. Homeless don't mean anything to me. I could sleep on the ground in the park and it wouldn't mean anything to me. I ain't homeless, I'm hopeless. I don't see a way to do anything better."

"That's why you got all this crack out here," Preacher said. "People know they in trouble and can't see a thing to do about it. Then they get into that crack and make believe they don't know what's happening to them."

"They know if they want to know," Sweeby said.

"All I know," the man sitting in Preacher's chair said, "was I come in here an hour ago for a haircut and I got to sit here and listen to all this talk instead of going home and spending some quality time with my family. I told you I was in a hurry."

"Man, your hair's been growing every minute you been here. It's just about all I can do to keep up with it. You lucky I'm not falling behind!"

"What you think about the garden?" Darnell asked Sweeby. "You want it?"

"Yes, I do," Sweeby said. "It'll be good for the people who don't have regular meals, and so on, and then it'll be good for the kids to see a different side of things."

"You were in the Army with my father, right?" Darnell asked.

"Twenty-fourth Transportation Battalion," Sweeby said.

"How come he did all right?"

" 'Cause he did the right things," Sweeby said. "He just found the right thing, or somebody told him the right thing, or he just knew the right thing. If he didn't get into the post office, I don't know what he would have done. But the post office ain't big enough for everybody."

"Post office is a nice job," Preacher said. "You got to be lucky to get into it. You got to find out when the test is being given, then you got to pass it high enough to be called."

"And you got to have an address so they can mail you a letter saying you passed the test," Sweeby said.

"You happy with your life?" Darnell asked.

"It could be better," Sweeby said. "But God gave me fifty-one years so far, so how can I complain?"

"Hard luck is better than no luck," Preacher said. "Down in Waycross, Georgia, they tell this story about a old black farmer who was working a tenant farm—"

"Man, are you ever going to finish this haircut?" Preacher's customer asked, annoyed.

"You better shut up before I raise the prices," Preacher said. "Anyway, he was complaining about how hard life was plowing behind the mule ten hours a day for a ten percent share of that farm. Every day he walked down each row and complained to the Lord about how hard he had it. One day just as he reached the end of a row the angel of death showed up and said he had come to take him out his misery.

" 'Misery? That ain't me complaining,' he said. 'That's the mule!'

"Angel of death struck the mule dead, and that's why you go down to Waycross today you can see an old fool plowing up a field all by his lonesome and just smiling to beat the band!"

Darnell smiled. "I guess that's the end of the interview."

"You supposed to turn it over to your anchorman and he's supposed to tell us what's going to be on the late news," Preacher said. "Hey, anchorman, what you got for the late news?"

"The lottery!" Larry said.

"I can deal with it," Preacher said. "I can deal with it."

Darnell shook hands with Sweeby, Preacher, and

the other two men in the barbershop, and so did Larry.

The sun was brighter than it had been when Darnell and Larry had gone into the barbershop, and there were long, black shadows across the sidewalk.

"How you think it went?" Larry asked.

"Okay, but a little bit scary," Darnell said.

"Scary?"

"They were all talking like the same things happened to them," Darnell said. "Then Sweeby got homeless. Even though he said he's not. How come if the same things happened to them it was just Sweeby that got homeless? I still didn't figure that out, and that's scary."

"Yeah," Larry said. "I guess."

TEN

What are we going to do about the homeless? We have to do something and we should do it soon. If we don't, things will just get worse.

Darnell looked at the words he had written. It was his fifth try, and he still didn't like it. He tore the paper out of the typewriter, crumpled it, and tossed it into the trash can. Mrs. Seldes had said he could do it, but he knew in his heart that he didn't believe it. Slowly he picked up a new sheet of blank paper and put it into the typewriter.

Sweeby Jones is a homeless man who deserves to have a decent place to live and something to eat every day. All human beings deserve this. So what we can do to help is to make . . .

He got up from his chair and fell heavily across the bed. He tried to clear his mind, to think of something else for a while instead of the article. He heard

the front doorbell ring, and a moment later,
Tamika's voice. He got up to open his door.

"Hey, Tamika, how's Molly?" he called.

"Not too good," Tamika said. "They think she's
going to have to go to the hospital to have her blood
cleaned."

"What?"

"Her kidneys don't work right," Tamika said. "So
she has to go to the hospital and they put her blood
through this machine that cleans it."

"That sounds rough."

"She said if she don't she could die." Tamika took
her jacket off and threw it on Darnell's bed. "How
you doing with your article?"

"So far it stinks," Darnell said. "I shouldn't have
let Miss Seldes talk me into this mess."

"She talked you into it?"

"She talked me into interviewing Sweeby."
Darnell took Tamika's jacket off his bed and threw it
across a chair. "The guy from the city paper wanted
to do the interview. What's that smell?"

"I put cocoa butter on my elbows because they
were getting rough," Tamika said.

"You just put cocoa butter on because you saw
Mama doing it," Darnell said.

"Why don't you call Miss Seldes and . . ."
Tamika looked into Darnell's trash can and saw all
the balled-up papers. She picked one up and read it.
"This isn't so bad," she said.

"It's not that good, either," Darnell said. "I can't
talk about it as good as Sweeby did. I played his tape
and it sounded important. But when I was trying to

make it sound important in writing, it came out funny."

"Why don't you just write down what he said?" Tamika asked. "Or call Miss Seldes and see what she says?"

"Maybe," Darnell said.

Tamika went to her room to start her homework, and Darnell looked at the paper he had just put into the machine. He looked at his homework assignment, decided to do it later, and closed his notebook.

The telephone was in the hall between his room and Tamika's. Darnell looked through the telephone book until he found Miss Seldes's number, and then dialed it. He thought she would probably be mad that he even called. He thought twice about hanging up before he heard her voice.

"Susan Seldes."

"Miss Seldes, this is Darnell. You know, from school?"

"Hello, Darnell." Miss Seldes had a pleasant voice.

"I'm just having a lot of trouble with this article," Darnell said. "I interviewed the guy—his name is Sweeby—but I can't seem to get the writing to sound like anything."

"How did the interview go?"

"Good," Darnell said.

"Then why don't you just run the interview?" Miss Seldes said.

"I was thinking about that," Darnell said.

"You have to edit it, of course," Miss Seldes continued. "You know, take out what's not relevant to the subject."

"Okay." Darnell picked up the telephone book and threw it toward Tamika's door. "Thanks a lot," he added, before hanging up.

"What's up?" Tamika asked.

"Miss Seldes said I should just use the interview."

"That's what I said." Tamika put her hand on her hip. "You have any more problems, you just come to Miss Tamika."

"You want to type it up for me?"

"What's in it for me?" Tamika asked.

"What do you want?"

"Go to the hospital with me tomorrow to see Molly Matera—"

"Uh-uh. Can't stand hospitals."

"Uh-uh." Tamika shook her head. "Can't stand typing."

"What time we going?"

It rained the next day and Jessica Lee and Mark got into an argument in front of the school about whether it could snow before December.

"That's why everybody is always wondering if there's going to be a white Christmas," Mark said, shaking his head slightly as he spoke.

"It can snow in August if it wanted to," Jessica said. "All it has to do is get cold enough."

"It can't get cold enough in August," Mark said, looking around for support. "Everybody knows that."

Darnell had already taken one copy of the interview that Tamika had typed up to the *Gazette* office, and his father had dropped off another copy at the *Oakdale Journal.*

"I'm proud of you, boy," he had said.

The argument between Jessica and Mark was getting stupid, and most of the kids were leaving. He was about to leave when he felt a nudge in the small of his back. It was Sonia Burrows.

"Hey, don't be nudging me in the back," Darnell said. "I started to turn around and give you a karate chop!"

"I got some news about the farming thing," Sonia said. "Let's go up to the class."

"The bell didn't ring yet," Darnell said. "They won't let us in."

"Then come around to the side of the building," Sonia said.

It was pretty cool, even though the sun was shining. Darnell followed Sonia around to the side of the building, watching her wade almost ankle deep through the autumn leaves. Along the hurricane fence at the side of the building, leaves were piling in small mounds, as if trying to escape from South Oakdale Middle School. The thought of leaves trying to escape school made Darnell smile.

"So what did you find out?" he asked when Sonia stopped and leaned against a tree.

"You know the guy who fills out prescriptions at the drugstore?"

"Tall, skinny guy?" Darnell pictured the druggist in his white coat.

"Yeah," Sonia said. "Well, he's a friend of my father and he was raised on a farm. He said that it's really hard to grow food in the city because the dirt hasn't been cared for. But he thinks the college would help out. They have people over there who know a lot about horticulture. You know what that is?"

"Farming?"

"Yeah, more or less," Sonia said. "Anyway, he gave me his name and everything and said to call him if he can help. He said he read about you in the paper. He asked were you really smart."

"Why did he ask that?"

"He wanted to know, I guess," Sonia said, smiling. "I told him you were pretty smart."

Darnell's first class today was supposed to be library and his second class was supposed to be English. He had planned to do his English homework in library, so when Mrs. Finley announced that they were going to have English first and then library, he knew he was going to get into trouble. He had spent the whole evening working on his article about Sweeby and hadn't written the book report that was due. His only hope was that she wouldn't check homework.

"Is there anybody here who has not done the book report?" Mrs. Finley asked.

Two hands went up quickly, and then three more went up slowly. Eddie Latimer held up his hand but tried to hide it behind the girl in front of him.

"Darnell, did you do the report?" Mrs. Finley asked.

"What report?" he asked.

He knew what report she meant, but couldn't think of anything else to say.

Mrs. Finley didn't answer him. She just looked at him, and then at the other kids who hadn't done their homework.

"Darnell, I had begun to expect a little more from you," she said.

"Can I bring it in tomorrow?" he asked.

"You had better bring it in tomorrow," Mrs. Finley said. "The best grade anyone can get on their report who has not finished it today is a 'C.' If you don't have it tomorrow you will get an 'F.' Is there anyone here who doesn't understand that?"

In the library Darnell found a copy of *The Old Man and the Sea* and looked to see if he could find his place. The old man seemed poor and maybe a little desperate, Darnell thought. He tried to imagine how he felt when the fish were eating the big fish he had caught. Darnell knew the old man must have felt like they were eating his whole life. He thought he understood the story pretty well. He got out his notebook and began to write. He had just finished when library period was over and he gave his pages to Mrs. Finley.

Darnell was going to his locker when Miss Joyner spoke to him in the hallway.

"Hello!" She was smiling as if she were really glad to see him. "Do you have a minute?"

"Yeah." He shrugged.

Miss Joyner looked around, and then motioned for Darnell to go into the science lab. She closed the door behind them and asked how he was doing.

"Fine," he answered.

"I just wanted to let you know that I have nothing against homeless people," Miss Joyner said. "I think we both believe it's right for us to help those who have difficulties helping themselves. But I think some ideas of how to do that are better than others. You understand that, don't you?"

"Yes." Darnell looked at Miss Joyner, wondering why she was talking to him.

"Okay. I just wanted to let you know how I felt," she said.

She smiled again, and then opened the door to the science lab. She left first and went down the hall, her heels clicking on the hard floor.

"Hey, Darnell, what you doing in there with Miss Joyner?" It was Chris McKoy. Angie Cruz slowed down as she was passing, and Darnell knew she was listening.

"I was checking out how she kissed," Darnell said. "She ain't bad for a teacher."

Chris gave him five and Angie turned just enough for him to see that she had a disgusted look on her face.

Tamika was waiting for him after school and gave him her books to carry as they went to the bus that would take them to the hospital to visit Molly Matera. The hospital was big and cold-looking on the outside, but inside it seemed friendly. There were yellow and white gladiola in the center of the circular lobby. On one side of the lobby there was a gift shop with little stuffed animals in the window. They stopped at the desk on the first floor to get passes, and a thin, dark woman wearing a badge that read "volunteer" asked them how old they were.

"Sixteen," Tamika said without hesitating.

"Are you sure?" the woman asked.

"Would this face lie to you?" Tamika pointed toward her face and smiled.

The woman gave them two passes.

Molly Matera, when she was healthy, had skin that was just about golden in color. But now that she was ill it was a dull tan. She had a wide mouth that she pulled into a weak smile when she saw Tamika and Darnell. Molly was up and playing solitaire when they arrived. She put the cards down and gave Tamika a hug.

"I had to bring Darnell because I promised my mother I would baby-sit," Tamika said.

"Hi, Darnell." Molly's voice was weak.

"How you doing?"

"Pretty good," Molly said. "All the tests came back okay. So I have to stay here until tomorrow, and then I have to come back once a month to go on a dialysis machine."

"That's the machine that cleans your blood?" Darnell asked.

"Yeah."

"Man, I'm sure glad that's not me!" Darnell heard himself blurting out.

"I don't blame you," Molly said. "I figured you had to do something to get sick like this. I didn't do anything."

"You got to get back to school and check out the happenings," Tamika said.

"Anything going on?"

"Just the fact that Angie Cruz is now liking Eddie Latimer!" Tamika said.

"Get out of here! I just spoke to her two days ago," Molly said. "She said she can't stand him!"

"Right, she can't stand him," Tamika said. "That's why she goes all over the school after him and they have fights about little stupid stuff."

"It sounds like the same old thing," Molly said.

The conversation between Tamika and Molly got worse than boring, and Darnell looked out the window. He was sorry he had said it, but he was glad he didn't have to have his blood cleaned by a machine. He was also glad he wasn't homeless.

On the way out he started to explain to Tamika about being sorry that he had said he was glad he didn't have to have his blood cleaned, but Tamika was mad and just looked away.

"Yo, anybody can make a mistake," he said.

"Our parents sure did when they had you," Tamika answered.

ELEVEN

★ The first thing that happened in the assembly was that Colin Rigby, who was holding the flag for the pledge of allegiance, tore the curtain with the point on top of the flagpole. That didn't get Mr. Baker mad, but when Chris McKoy started laughing, Mr. Baker got mad. He warned Chris that he would put him out if he didn't keep quiet.

Next the whole assembly started laughing when Mr. Baker announced that no girls could go into the boys' locker room.

"That's sexist!" Linda Gold called out.

"Do you want boys to come into the girls' locker room?" Mr. Baker's neck was swelling up the way it always did when he was mad.

"I don't care!" she said.

Then a lot of the boys started making noises like "wooo-wooo!" and a few whistles. Naturally, Chris McKoy made the most noise, and that was when Mr. Baker threw him out of the assembly.

As Chris started out, he was still laughing. Darnell was smiling as he watched Chris go, and then something that Sweeby said came to him. Sweeby had said that when he went to school he didn't know what to do, he just did what everybody expected him to do. That's what Chris was doing, too. Everybody expected him to act stupid, to pretend that school was a joke, and that's what he did.

An image of Sweeby came to Darnell. He wondered if Sweeby had thought that school was a joke. One thing he did know, that the distance between Sweeby and Chris was becoming less.

Mr. Baker announced that the whole school was going to have reading tests after Thanksgiving, and he expected everyone to do well.

"The only thing you have to worry about on these tests is doing your best," he said. "Sometimes I don't think young people realize the importance of the testing program. But if you do your best, not only on the tests, but also on the practice tests that your teacher will give you, you'll be okay."

Mr. Baker handed the microphone to Mrs. Finley and started to leave when Chris McKoy came back into the assembly.

"Hey, there's a dog in the hallway!" he called out.

Everyone turned around and looked at Chris and started laughing.

Mr. Baker's neck got bigger and his mouth tightened.

"What kind of dog?" he asked Chris.

"A big dog!" Chris said, laughing.

Mr. Derby and Mr. Thrush went into the hall to look for the dog. When they came back, they said they didn't see any dog. Mr. Baker told Chris to report to his office after school.

Darnell walked with Angie as they left the assembly. She seemed annoyed, almost mad. It was about Linda.

"She doesn't want to go into the boys' locker room." Angie pushed her glasses up on her nose. "What she really wants to do is have everybody notice her."

"All the boys are going to notice her if she comes into the locker room," Darnell said. "And she's going to notice them."

Just then Paula came running out of the girls' bathroom screaming that the dog was in there.

Mr. Derby asked if there were any girls in the bathroom.

"I don't think so," Paula said.

Mr. Derby went in as a group of kids gathered around the outside of the bathroom. He came out a minute later with a small brown puppy. All the girls started oohing and aahing, and the boys started laughing.

"That's what you should be writing about," Linda said. "Dogs going into the bathroom. You probably know something about that!"

"What's that supposed to mean?" Darnell asked.

"It means that the school newspaper is supposed to be serious," Linda replied, raising her voice. "You're not supposed to write just anything that comes into your head. And tell me, Mr. Know-So-Much, just what do those guys hanging out on the street corners know about making a garden? What do *you* know about making a garden? You can't grow vegetables just by throwing seeds on the ground. So what do they know about it?"

"They know as much as you do," Darnell answered.

"Right, which is why I buy my food from the supermarket," Linda snapped. "The mayor and the City Council can't even solve the homeless problem. How are you going to solve it?"

"What are you trying to solve by going into the boys' locker room?" Darnell asked. "You got a sex problem or something?"

"That's a *real* issue," Linda said. "They let women reporters go into the locker rooms in the major leagues and in the National Football League. Or don't you and your Corner Crew even read the papers?"

"Hey, don't be telling me about reading the papers," Darnell said.

"Don't *be* telling me?" Linda's voice was really sarcastic. "I won't *be* telling you anything. But I will *be* writing an article about your stupid idea for a garden. Then we'll see who writes the best. And who do you think that will be?"

"Me!" Darnell said.

"Hah!" Linda answered. She started laughing as she walked away.

"I feel like punching her in her mouth," Darnell said.

"You punch her and I'll write up the story for the paper," Angie said.

Math was the next class, but Darnell couldn't get

his mind off Linda. Mr. Ohrbach called on him four times and he didn't know the answers. He had never had anybody just walk up to him and put him down like that unless that person was a lot bigger than he was, and a guy.

He tried to get his mind on what Mr. Ohrbach was saying, but he kept thinking about Linda. He thought again about hitting her but knew that if he did he would just get into trouble.

One of the things he had found out was that everybody had an opinion about homeless people and they got mad when you said something they didn't like.

He finally got his mind off Linda and started thinking about a program he had seen on television the week before. It was a cartoon he and Tamika had been watching in which some kind of superhero was chasing a bad guy in a spaceship. In the cartoon the bad guy wanted the hero to get close enough to capture him because he had a trap. Darnell ran the whole cartoon in his mind as if it were a movie he could play anytime he wanted, and forced himself to do it over and over again until the end of the period.

In the hallway Chris was trying to get people to sign a petition so that he wouldn't have to serve detention.

"There *was* a dog in the hallway!" he was saying.

"Who let him in the girls' bathroom?" Darnell asked.

"He went in there looking for Linda," Chris said.

"Can I quote you on that?" Tony O! put his hand up for a high five, and Chris slapped it.

Then Tony O! saw Paula and asked about the social studies homework.

Tony O! had laughed and Chris had laughed, but when Darnell walked away only Chris was still laughing.

Tamika found Darnell near the water cooler and told him that she was going to Molly Matera's house after school, and for him to tell their mother.

"She say you could go?" Darnell asked.

"I told her I might go and she said to tell you so you could tell her," Tamika said.

"You hear about me and Linda?"

"Yeah!" Tamika smiled. "You want me to punch her lights out?"

"I don't need you to fight my battles," Darnell said.

"She's just jealous because you're getting more attention than she is," Tamika said. "She wouldn't even care if the homeless people got a garden or not if you didn't get so much attention. And she would have loved it if it was her idea."

"Hey, I guess some of us have it, and some of us don't," Darnell said.

"Yeah, you may write a good story, but you're still ugly."

"Get out of here."

Tamika took the Westgate bus, the one that went past Molly's house, and Darnell started walking home. He thought about Sweeby and Chris, and how they were connected in a way. Then he thought

about his report on *The Old Man and the Sea,* and
wondered again why it happened that the fish at-
tacked the old man's fish and he couldn't do anything about it. For a moment he stopped and
thought about how maybe Sweeby was like the old
man in the story, but then he knew he wasn't. The
old man had caught a fish and wanted everybody to
know how good a fisherman he was. The fish was
really big and he had tied it to the boat to take back
to show the people who laughed at him, but the
other fish had eaten it. Darnell felt sorry for the old
man, but he had done something and it just hadn't
worked out. But Sweeby hadn't done anything that
hadn't worked out that he knew about.

Darnell reached Fairview Avenue, but instead of
turning left he turned right and walked up the street
to Jackson. It was windy and there were a few drops
of rain in the gusts that blew into his face. He
searched the streets, looking at the shapes of the
men standing on the corners, until he found the one
he wanted.

"You come back to interview me again?"

"What was the biggest thing you tried that
failed?" Darnell asked.

"The biggest thing I tried?" Sweeby ran his finger-
tips over the stubble on his chin. Then he nudged
the man next to him. "Tried to fly to the moon one
time," he said. "But my retrorockets weren't working that day, so I took me a walk around the block
instead!"

The two men laughed, and in spite of himself,
Darnell laughed, too.

"Did you ever go back to school?" Darnell asked.

"Now how would I look going back to school at my age?" Sweeby's voice had an edge to it. "If that's the best you can do, you better take up some other profession."

"Yeah." Darnell shrugged.

The walk home seemed short. When he got there he told his mother that Tamika was going to see Molly.

"Her mother called and told me," his mother said. "You hungry?"

"Sort of."

"Dinner will be ready in about ten minutes."

Darnell went to the phone in the hall. The directory was in the shelf under it. He looked up a number and called it.

"Hello? Is this the *Oakdale Journal*?"

The voice on the other end said that it was, and Darnell asked for the editor. He needed to make some changes in the story he had written.

TWELVE

 Someone knocked on the door at six-thirty in the morning. Mrs. Rock and Tamika were sitting at the kitchen table.

"I bet it's Larry," Tamika said.

"Not this early." Mrs. Rock got up and went to the door. She looked through the peephole, then unlocked and opened the door.

"Good morning!" Mrs. Rock nodded to Mr. Green, the building's superintendent.

"Just thought you'd want to see this." Mr. Green handed Mrs. Rock a copy of the *Oakdale Journal*. "I always knew that boy would be something."

By the time Mrs. Rock had thanked Mr. Green for bringing up the paper, Tamika had run into Darnell's bedroom and shaken him. It took less than a minute for him to get into the kitchen.

"What's going on out here?" Mr. Rock came out in his bathrobe.

"Darnell's article is in the *Journal* today," Mrs.

Rock said. "Mr. Green brought it up. Here it is. Tamika, read it aloud!"

Tamika looked at the article, nudged Darnell, and started reading.

"Nobody wants to be homeless," Sweeby Jones said. He is a homeless man who lives in our city of Oakdale. It is for him and people like him that I think we should build a garden where the basketball courts were, near the school. That way the homeless people can help themselves by raising food.

"You see a man or woman that's hungry and you don't feed them, or help them feed themselves, then you got to say you don't mind people being hungry," Mr. Jones said. "And if you don't mind people being hungry, then there is something wrong with you."

This is what Mr. Sweeby Jones said when I spoke to him. I don't want to be the kind of person who says it's all right for some people to be hungry. I want to do something about it. But I think there is another reason to have the garden. Things can happen to people that they don't plan. You can get sick, and not know why, or even homeless. But sometimes there are things you can do to change your life or make it good. If you don't do anything to make your life good, it will probably not be good.

"I was born poor and will probably be poor all my life," Mr. Sweeby Jones said.

I think maybe it is not how you were born that makes the most difference, but what you do with your life. The garden is a chance for some people to help their own lives.

Darnell Rock is a seventh-grader at South Oakdale Middle School. The school board has proposed that the site that Mr. Rock wants to make into a garden be used as a parking lot for teachers. The City Council will decide the issue tomorrow evening.

"I think that's a good article, Darnell!" Mr. Rock said.

"I typed it up," Tamika said. "Only the newspaper must have added that little bit about the City Council."

"You got it just right," Mr. Rock said. "Anybody can become homeless. You got to give people a chance."

"That's really not what I thought I said," Darnell said.

"I can't become homeless because I'm too cute," Tamika said. "When you ever see anybody as cute as me being homeless?"

"What you think, Mom?"

Mrs. Rock sat at the table and picked up her coffee cup. The coffee had now grown cold. "I think I can see what you're saying," Mrs. Rock said. "You're saying that being homeless doesn't just 'happen' to people. I think I'll have to think about it for a while. It's a good article, but I'll think about it some more and let you know."

"I'm going to ask Mr. Baker if I can read it during announcements," Tamika said.

THIRTEEN

Six kids on the school bus had copies of the *Journal*, and everybody had read Darnell's article by the time the bus pulled up to South Oakdale Middle School. When Darnell and Tamika got off the bus, they saw four other kids reading the paper. Tamika took her copy of the *Journal* to a group of her friends.

"Way to go, Darnell!" Benny called from the front steps.

Darnell felt like a celebrity.

"Yo, Darnell." Tony O! came up to him and handed him two typed sheets. "Check out Linda's article. She made copies and she's passing them out to everybody. She's got her friends saying her article is better than yours. No way!"

Darnell didn't read the article until he reached homeroom.

```
Teaching is a difficult profession.
Teachers need as much support as they
can possibly get. After all, we are de-
pendent on them for our future. Educa-
```

tion is the key to a good and secure future, and teachers help us to get that education. We must give them all the support we can. This is why I am supporting the idea of building a parking lot near the school.

There are some people in our school who think it is a good idea to build a garden so that the homeless can use it. Use it for what? Homeless people don't have experience farming and could not use the land anyway. This is just a bad idea that will help nobody and will hurt the teachers. The teachers give us good examples on how we should live and how we should conduct ourselves. The homeless people, even though it is no fault of theirs, don't give us good examples.

On Friday evening, at 7:00 p.m., the City Council will meet to make a final decision. I urge them to support the teachers, support education, and support the students at South Oakdale.

"I think Linda's article was better than yours," Chris McKoy said later as they sat in the corner of the lunchroom. There were at least twenty kids gathered around their table. On the other side of the room there was another group, sitting around Linda's table. "In the first place, she's got that stuff in it about education, and you don't."

"I don't see how parking a car is about education," Larry said.

"That doesn't mean anything," Chris said. "When you're writing something you got to bring all that kind of stuff in it."

"I liked Darnell's article," Fred Haskell said. "Mostly because he used quotes. He's got what he thinks in his article and what that guy thinks. But what kind of name is Sweeby?"

"It's just a name," Tony O! said. "And I like your article better, Darnell, because it's not sucking up to the teachers."

"But she's still right," Chris said. "We're supposed to be here for education and stuff, not to feed people."

"So you think it's okay to have people hungry and homeless?" Sonia asked.

"It's not my business," Chris said. "I didn't tell them to be homeless."

"Then if you mess up," Darnell said, "it's okay for you to be homeless, right?"

"I'm not going to mess up!" Chris said.

"You messed up already," Tony O! said.

"Suppose I mess up your face!" Chris said, standing. He grabbed Tony O! by the shirt and pulled him across the table.

"Hey, man, he's just talking like everybody else," Darnell said.

Chris pushed Tony O! away.

The first bell rang, and kids started to leave the lunchroom. Chris brushed by Tony O! on the way out and knocked his books out of his hand. Tony O!

left the books on the floor until Chris had left the lunchroom, then started picking them up. Darnell saw that his eyes were glistening.

"Here comes Linda." Sonia looked down at her hands.

Darnell put his milk container and silverware on his tray as he waited for Linda to get to his table. Out of the corner of his eye he saw that there were a couple of people with her.

"I read your article," Jessica Lee said as she, Linda, and Mark reached Darnell's table. "I thought it was kind of stupid."

"That's your opinion," Darnell said.

"Are you coming to the City Council meeting tomorrow night?" Linda asked. "All you have to do is put your name in and you can speak. You can read your article."

"I might come," Darnell said.

"Good, I'll see you there." Linda smiled.

In gym they had aerobics for ten minutes, and then free play. They played H-O-R-S-E for a while and then got into a three-on-three game. The game was on for less than a minute before Chris got into an argument with Tony O!

Tony O! stood up to Chris, but Darnell knew that there was no way he was going to beat Chris in a fight. Chris kept calling Tony O! a punk, and Tony O! called Chris a turkey. Then Chris pushed Tony O!

The push wasn't that hard, but Tony O! reached out to push Chris back. That's when Chris punched Tony O! in the face. Tony O! grabbed the side of his face and turned away as Mr. Day started blowing his whistle.

Darnell watched as Mr. Day rushed across the gym, where the boys had formed a circle around Tony O! and Chris. Mr. Day grabbed Chris by the collar and dragged him over to the bleachers. He pushed Chris against the bleachers.

"You just stay there!" Mr. Day yelled.

He went back to where Darnell was trying to get Tony O! to move his hand from his face so he could see how bad he was hurt.

Mr. Day grabbed Tony O!'s wrist and moved it.

Tony O!'s eye was red and already starting to puff up. Mr. Day told Larry to go to the nurse with Tony O!, then went back to Chris and told him to follow him.

As Mr. Day stalked out of the gym with Chris behind him, Darnell knew that they were headed toward Mr. Baker's office.

After school Larry found Darnell and told him that Tony O! had gone home after seeing the school nurse.

"His eye didn't look that bad," Larry said. "But he was mad. He was talking about taking out a contract on Chris."

"Chris shouldn't have hit him." Darnell looked away. He saw that the trees had lost most of their leaves.

"I think he don't think much if a teacher tells him he's messed up," Larry said. "But he don't like it if another kid tells him."

"Linda told him he was and he didn't say anything," Darnell answered.

"Linda and you aren't regular kids," Larry said.

"What you mean, I'm not regular?"

"Everybody's talking about you," Larry said.

"That's funny," Darnell answered. "You can say something and it doesn't mean much. You put it in the newspaper and all of a sudden everybody is getting all excited."

"Aren't you excited about it?" Larry asked.

"Yeah," Darnell said. "I guess I am."

FOURTEEN

 "You see anybody from the school?" Larry looked over the large crowd at the Oakdale Court building.

"There goes Mr. Derby *and* Mr. Baker." Tamika pointed toward the front of the building.

Darnell felt a lump in the pit of his stomach. There were at least a hundred people at the City Council meeting.

Tamika led them through the crowd to where she had spotted Mr. Derby and South Oakdale's principal. The large, high-ceilinged room had rows of benches that faced the low platform for the City Council. Linda Gold was already sitting in the front row. Darnell saw that her parents were with her.

He had brought a copy of the *Journal* with him and saw that a few other people, grown-ups, also had copies of the paper.

The nine members of the City Council arrived, and the meeting was called to order. The city clerk said that there were five items on the agenda, and read them off. The first three items were about

Building Code violations. Then came something about funding the city's library.

"The last item will be the use of the basketball courts as a parking lot at South Oakdale Middle School," the clerk said. "We have three speakers scheduled."

Linda turned and smiled at Darnell.

"You want me to run up there and punch her out?" Tamika whispered to Darnell.

Darnell didn't know what Building Code violations were but watched as building owners showed diagrams explaining why there were violations. The first two weren't that interesting, but the third one was. A company had built a five-story building that was supposed to be a minimum of twenty feet from the curb, but it was only fifteen feet.

"You mean to tell me that your engineers only had fifteen-foot rulers?" one councilman asked.

"Well, er, we measured it right the first time"—the builder shifted from one foot to the other—"but then we made some changes in the design and somehow we sort of forgot about the er . . . you know . . . the other five feet."

To Darnell the builder sounded like a kid in his homeroom trying to make an excuse for not having his homework.

"Can you just slide the building back five or six feet?" the councilman asked.

Everybody laughed and the builder smiled, but Darnell could tell he didn't think it was funny.

Somebody touched Darnell on the shoulder, and he turned and saw his parents.

"We have this ordinance for a reason," a woman on the Council was saying. "I don't think we should lightly dismiss this violation. An exception granted here is just going to encourage others to break the law."

"This is going to ruin me," the builder said. "I've been in Oakdale all of my life and I think I've made a contribution."

"Let's have a vote." The head of the Council spoke sharply.

"Let's have a vote to postpone a decision," the woman who had spoken before said. "We'll give Mr. Miller an opportunity to show his good faith."

"What do you want me to do?" the builder asked.

"That's up to you," the woman said.

"Next time you'd better get it right!" Tamika called out.

"She's right," the councilwoman said.

There was a vote, and the decision was postponed. The builder gave Tamika a dirty look as he pushed his papers into his briefcase.

The city library funding was next, and eight people, including Miss Seldes, spoke for the library, but the Council said it didn't have any more money. There was some booing, including some from Tamika and Larry. Darnell knew that if he didn't have to speak he would have enjoyed the meeting.

"The issue at South Oakdale is should the old basketball courts be used as a parking lot, or should they be used as a community garden?"

"Who's going to pay for paving the lot?" a councilman asked. "Does it have to be paved?"

"It's my understanding that it doesn't have to be paved," the head of the Council answered. "Am I right on that?"

"Yes, you are," Miss Joyner spoke up from the audience.

"We have two young people from the school to speak," the councilwoman said. "The first is a Miss Gold."

Linda went into the middle aisle, where there was a microphone. She began reading her article in the snootiest voice that Darnell had ever heard. He felt a knot in his stomach. He turned to look at his mother, and she was smiling. On the stage some of the councilmen were looking at some papers.

"I hope I don't mess up," he whispered to Tamika.

"You won't," Tamika said.

Linda finished reading her article and then turned toward Darnell.

"Although everybody would like to help the homeless," she said, "schools are supposed to be for kids, and for those who teach kids! Thank you."

There was applause for Linda, and Miss Joyner stood up and nodded toward her. Darnell felt his hands shaking.

Darnell's name was called, and he made the long trip to the microphone.

"When I first thought about having a garden instead of a parking lot, I thought it was just a good idea," Darnell said. "Then, when the *Journal* asked me to send them a copy of my interview with Mr. Jones, I was thinking that it was mainly a good idea to have a garden to help out the homeless people.

But now I think it might be a good idea to have the garden to help out the kids—some of the kids—in the school.

"Sometimes, when people go through their life they don't do the things that can make them a good life. I don't know why they don't do the right thing, or maybe even if they know what the right thing is sometimes.

"But I see the same thing in my school, South Oakdale. Some of the kids always do okay, but some of us don't. Maybe their parents are telling them something, or maybe they know something special. But if you're a kid who isn't doing so good, people start off telling you what you should be doing, and you know it, but sometimes you still don't get it done and mess up some more. Then people start expecting you to mess up, and then *you* start expecting you to mess up. Teachers get mad at you, or the principal, or your parents, and they act like you're messing up on purpose. Like you want to get bad marks and stuff like that. Then you don't want people getting on your case all the time so you don't do much because the less you do the less they're going to be on your case. Only that doesn't help anything, and everybody knows it, but that's the way it goes."

"You seem to be doing all right, young man," the head of the City Council said.

"I wasn't doing too hot before," Darnell said, taking a quick look over to where Mr. Baker sat. "But when I got on the paper and the *Journal* printed my article, then everybody started treating me different. People came up to me and started explaining their points of view instead of just telling me what to do. And you people are listening to me. The kids I hung out with, they called us the Corner Crew, are mostly good kids but you wouldn't listen to them unless they got into trouble.

"In South Oakdale some kids have bad things happen to them—like they get sick—and I don't know why that happens, but all they can do is to go to the hospital. And some kids just get left out of the good things and can't find a way of getting back into them. People get mad at them the same way they get mad at the homeless people or people who beg on the street. Maybe the garden will be a way for the homeless people to get back into some good things, and maybe seeing the homeless people getting back into a better life will be a way for some of the kids to think about what's happening to them. Thank you."

There was some applause as Darnell turned to go back to his seat.

"Just a minute, young man," one of the councilmen called to him. "The girl said that these people don't know anything about raising a garden. Is that true?"

"It doesn't matter," someone said from the audience. "I'm from the college, and we can help with technical advice."

"I didn't ask you," the councilman said.

"I'm telling you anyway," the man said.

"I don't know how effective a community garden would be," the councilman said. "You can't feed people from a garden."

"You could sell what you grow," Darnell heard himself saying.

"I think bringing people who are . . . nonschool people into that close a contact with children might not be that good an idea," the councilman said. "Who's the last speaker?"

"A Mr. Jones," the clerk said.

Sweeby came into the middle aisle, and a lot of people began to talk among themselves. There were a lot of things they were interested in, and most of them were not interested in the school parking lot.

"I just want to ask you why you don't want to listen to this boy," Sweeby asked.

"You have four minutes to speak," the councilman said. He seemed angry. "We don't have to answer your questions."

"You don't have to answer my questions," Sweeby said. "And you don't have to have the garden. You don't have to think about us—what you call us?—nonschool people?

"But it's a shame you don't want to listen to this boy. I wish he had been my friend when I was his age. Maybe I would be sitting in one of your seats instead of being over here."

"Is there anything more?" the councilman asked.

"No, you can just forget about the whole thing now," Sweeby said. "Go on back to your papers."

"I think we can vote on this issue now," the councilman said.

"I think Mr."—the councilman looked at the agenda to find Darnell's name—"Mr. Darnell Rock had some good points, but it's still a tough issue. Let's get on with the vote."

The vote went quickly. Three councilpeople decided not to vote, five voted against the garden, and only one voted for it.

Darnell took a deep breath and let it out slowly. Tamika patted him on his hand. When he looked at her she had tears in her eyes.

Darnell felt he had let Sweeby down. His father patted him on his back, and Miss Seldes came over.

"You did a good job," she said. "Really good."

"I lost," Darnell said.

"Sometimes you lose," Miss Seldes said. "But you still did a good job."

Sweeby and some of his friends were waiting outside the Council meeting, and they shook hands with Darnell. Sweeby was telling him how the members of the Council didn't really care about people when Darnell saw Linda through the crowd. She waved and he waved back. She was smiling.

Larry's mother came over and asked his father for a lift home, and they were waiting for Larry when Peter Miller from the *Journal* came over.

"Hey, you want to write another article for the paper?" he said. "There's a guy who wants to donate a couple of lots for a garden in another location. My boss wants to run it as a human interest piece."

"Yeah, sure," Darnell said. "You want a long article or a short one?"

"I don't know. Call the paper tomorrow and ask

for the city desk," the reporter said. "My editor will give you the word count."

"Okay," Darnell said. "But first I have to check with my editor to see what she wants."

FIFTEEN

★ Darnell was disappointed that the Jackson Avenue garden was as small as it was, but as Sweeby said, it was a start. It was located between two abandoned buildings and was fifty feet deep by thirty-five feet wide. A flatbed truck was parked in front of it and was being used as a platform for the mayor as he made his speech about how some kids from South Oakdale had "made things happen."

"And as long as I'm mayor, I'll always listen to the kids, for they are the future!" he said. Then he got down from the truck, got into a limousine, and was gone.

"They should have named it after you!" Larry said.

"When they name stuff after you it means you're dead!" Darnell said.

"Darnell!" It was Linda Gold.

"What?"

"They want you to be in a picture breaking the ground," Linda said.

"Doing what?"

"Breaking the ground," Linda said. "Just come over here and hold the shovel."

Linda reached over and took Darnell's hand and started toward where a small knot of reporters was gathered in one corner.

When they reached the reporters, Darnell was told to put his hand on the shovel.

"You the man of the hour," Sweeby said. He had his hand right next to Darnell's.

They all put one hand on the shovel, as if they were all digging with it at the same time, and had their picture taken. When that was finished, a reporter asked Sweeby how he felt.

"I feel good," Sweeby said. "A young brother like Darnell here has put his mind to a problem of his people. How you going to feel bad when something like that happens?"

"Do you really think this garden is going to make a difference?" the reporter asked.

"It's going to make a big difference," Sweeby said. "Because every time somebody walks by this place they're going to remember that there are people who need some help, and there are some people who are willing to help. You can't see that?"

"Yeah, I guess so," the reporter said, closing his notebook. He shook Sweeby's hand before walking away.

"Looka that," Sweeby said to Darnell after the reporter had left. "When's the last time you think he shook the hand of a used-to-be homeless man?"

"You got a place to stay now?" Darnell asked.

"You got me so excited about being down at the

City Council and in the newspapers that I had to do something," Sweeby said. "And me being in the newspapers helped because the hospital offered me a job. Like this garden, it's small, but it's a start. Now, you take care of yourself. I got about a half hour to get to work."

Sweeby started off with one of his friends, and Darnell started looking for Tamika.

It was Tamika who woke up Darnell on Saturday morning.

"Get up," she said. "Mama wants you to go get some bran flakes and a half gallon of low-fat milk."

"How come she wants me to go when you're up already?" Darnell asked.

"Because it looks like it might rain," Tamika said, "and she's afraid I might melt."

"Yeah, right!"

Darnell got up, dressed, and found that his mother did want him to go to the store for cereal, milk, and potatoes. Outside it was cool and raining lightly. A stray dog followed Darnell down the street, turning with him when he decided to go over to Jackson to take another look at the garden.

Mrs. Lucas from across the street walked over to him. "Hey, ain't you that little Rock boy?" Her hat was on crooked, and she looked mad when she talked, the way she always did.

"Yes, ma'am," Darnell answered without stopping.

"Don't you walk away from me like no fresh thing!" Mrs. Lucas called after him.

"I wasn't walking away." Darnell stopped.

"Well, you don't have those people raising no tomatoes," Mrs. Lucas said. "Those tomatoes get wormy they can kill you faster than take wings and fly!"

"Yes, ma'am," Darnell said.

"You go on," Mrs. Lucas said. "And you remember about them wormy tomatoes!"

Darnell started down the street again, the dog following him all the way. He stopped down the street from the garden. There was someone in it. It wasn't Sweeby, just an old man picking up handfuls of dirt and letting it run through his fingers.

"Hey, dog, what you think about the garden right here on Jackson Avenue?" Darnell asked the dog.

The dog looked at him, saw another kid walking down the other side of the street, and went to follow him.

Darnell went back to the supermarket. When he came out he saw Larry on his bicycle.

"Tamika said you were over here," Larry said.

"You want to carry this stuff on your bike?" Darnell asked.

They put the shopping bag on the crossbar and rolled the bike as they headed toward Darnell's house.

"So what you thinking about writing about next?" Larry asked.

"Wormy tomatoes," Darnell said. "They can kill you, man."

"No lie?"

"No lie!"

About the Author

Walter Dean Myers serves as the National Ambassador for Young People's Literature. He is a poet, a novelist, a playwright, and a musician. His books for young readers have received numerous awards, including two Newbery Honors, five Coretta Scott King Awards, five *Boston Globe–Horn Book* Honors, the Margaret A. Edwards Award, the first Michael L. Printz Award, the ALAN Award, and the Virginia Hamilton Award.

Walter Dean Myers grew up in New York City's Harlem. He lives in Jersey City, New Jersey.